Midley Abandoned

Emma Batten

All rights reserved

No part of this publication may be reproduced, stored in a retrieval system, or transmitted in any form or by any means without the prior permission in writing of the publisher, nor be otherwise circulated in any form of binding or cover other than that in which it is published and without a similar condition including this condition being imposed on the subsequent purchaser.

The moral right of the author has been asserted

First published in the UK by Emma Batten.

Edited by Debbie Rigden

Further editing and proofreading by Liz Hopkin & Maud Matley

Cover painting by Kean Farrelly

www.emmabattenauthor.com

For Debbie,

With thanks for all the inconsistencies you spot, your amazing ability to recall what I have, or have not, written in earlier chapters, and for sharing your local knowledge with me.

You have supported me and my writing from the very beginning, first as a reader and then editor, and I love working with you as each new story comes to life.

Introduction

Welcome back to my series of novellas inspired by church ruins at Midley, a lost village between Old Romney and Lydd. Having built the stone church in my last story, we now move forward two centuries. The hamlet of Midley never grew large enough or prosperous enough to sustain a church. Sadly, the building has deteriorated and become home to an unexpected (fictional) character.

The inspiration comes from Archbishop Parker's notes from his visit to Romney Marsh in 1573. All characters are fictional, other than Archbishop Parker. The farms Wheelsgate and Deanes are real places, but the current Deanes/Deans Court is a newer building. The rectory at Old Romney is a fictional property on the site of a later rectory, now called The Shrubbery. We visit Dengemarsh briefly. The farms mentioned are still there and the chapel did exist, but the description is imaginary.

I hope you enjoy this third story in the Midley series.

Lucy

Near Brookland, Romney Marsh 1573

"Lucy?" Mistress Ruth bellowed. "Lucy? Where are you, girl?"

As she thumped down the stairs, I raced into the larder, letting the door shut behind me with a clunk. I grinned, pleased to be free of her nagging, and placed a dish of butter on the stone shelf. A small window let in some light, and my gaze fell on a tempting piece of uncovered honey tart. Hoping no one would notice it missing, I started stuffing the sticky crumbs into my mouth.

A moment later, a latch clacked, the farmhouse door opened, and footsteps pounded on the dirt floor. This was followed by low thuds and a clatter, as something dropped onto the scrubbed table. I frowned, not recognising the sounds, but knowing the master was home and wouldn't think kindly of me hiding in the larder.

"What's them dirty old things?" Mistress Ruth asked, her voice a low whine.

"Have some respect, woman," Mister Walter snapped back at her. "It's the alms box, candlesticks and church plate."

"From where? It doesn't look like anything special."

I could picture the curl of her lip and couldn't help but feel curious.

"Midley. Now fetch me a basket to store them in. Tomorrow, I'll ask the girl to go over the pewter and give it a polish. Then you'll change your tune."

"Midley!" Mistress Ruth wailed. "That's where you've been all these hours. But why come back with these grubby old things? Church plate, you say. It's nothing but a cup and a dish, and as dull as can be. Who gave them to you? What are you going to do with them?"

"Too many questions," he bawled. "What's this?"

From my hide I heard a scraping sound. "I've got my needlework in there," the mistress whinged. "There's a blanket to patch and a shawl that's seen…"

"They can go in the trunk," the master said, sounding pleased with himself. "This basket will suit me nicely."

"But you still haven't said…"

"Because it's none of your damned business," he shouted. "I've been to look over the old place and it's going to ruin. There's no glass in the windows – God knows where it's gone – and half the floor tiles have been lifted. The wood is rotting, and the fencing has been taken."

I squatted on the larder floor, my back against the cold wall. From the kitchen there came the sound of the wicker basket being slammed down on the table, followed by the low thud of the wooden alms box, then the clatter of metal. *Please God, don't let Mistress Ruth come in here. Please God, send her out to collect the eggs or draw water from the well. Anything but come in here.* Although I was no stranger to them arguing, if they found me listening, I'd be in for a tongue-lashing from her, a clout from him, and no supper.

"It's not our church," Mistress Ruth grumbled. "It's never been mine and never yours either."

"It was my father's and his father's and all the others going back and back," he shouted. "So don't you go telling me what's mine and what's not. Someone should be looking after the old place. It's not right."

"There's no one left."

"So, I've taken these because if I don't, who's going to give them a polish and get the pewter shining again? And this box – look at the detail in the carving – it will go to rot if it's not cared for. I'll keep them nice and one day, when the archbishop comes along and says he'll get it all fixed up, they can go back."

"But you shouldn't have gone there. Not to the church and not gone and taken things to bring back here into our home."

"Why ever not?" he bellowed. "As long as you have wood for your fire and food in your belly, then you can thank the Lord that I treat you well and stop your nagging."

"Why not?" she whimpered. "Why not? Don't you know what they say about Midley – about the holy building?"

"What do they say?" he sneered.

"The body washer lives there. Right there in the church."

"The body washer?" he echoed. "Him who washes the bodies? In my church?"

"It's not strictly your church." Mistress Ruth never missed a chance to correct him. "Aye he's there."

"I didn't see him."

"He was out," she shrieked. "But it doesn't mean… it doesn't mean he's not there when he's not washing bodies. Now look what you've done with your interfering. You've brought a bit of Midley back here. A bit of the plague."

Silence fell between them, just for a moment. He must have been thinking about her words, and for once Mistress Ruth ceased the wagging of her tongue.

"I'll put them in the barn loft," he said. "It's dry up there. Where's the girl? My belly feels like it's been empty for a week. What's for supper?"

"There's a ham in the larder," she replied. "After we've eaten, I'll be going to pray – pray that He thinks to spare you. It would do no harm for you to come with me."

Ham in the larder! I leapt onto a crate, heaved myself up, and plunged through the window, scraping my arms and legs on the shutters. Falling to the ground, narrowly missing the master's cart, I came down hard on my right shoulder and heard the unmistakable creak of the larder door. There was no time to sit feeling sorry for myself; I knew the master would be rounding the corner of the house at any moment.

Before I scampered along to the vegetable plots, I heard the familiar whinging tone of Mistress Ruth: "Why's the larder window open?"

Peas. Peas. Must pick some peas, I told myself over and over while snatching at the pods, pulling at the plants and tearing them. But it was impossible – in my flustered state even this simple task was beyond me.

What does she mean? Who is he? Who is the body washer?

Lucy

Two days have passed since the master came back from Midley with the precious church plate and alms box. He and Mistress Ruth are both subdued, although sometimes she can't contain her natural urge to moan at him, and he can't help but bark back at her. I've not seen those holy pieces and neither have I been told to clean them as I heard him suggest. I think he put them in the barn loft, but I won't go looking up there.

Mister Walter has mostly been out in the fields with the sheep because of the young lambs. He has a looker settled in a hut over in the far fields near the little church – the one that sits surrounded by water most of the time. The master goes over there checking that all is well with the looker and the flock, then returns to keep an eye on the ewes closer to the farmhouse.

Sometimes we have an orphan or a weakling in the kitchen with us, but I don't mind, even though the mistress says I must feed it during the night. I'd rather that than have one of them coming down and disturbing me when I'm trying to sleep on my pallet.

Besides, I like having a little one to cuddle. One stayed for just a few nights this year and she's out in the fields now with the others.

On Sunday after church, Mistress Ruth lets me go to see my sister at Wheelsgate Farm. Kitty gets treated well there, and they don't mind me going in for a glass of milk. Sometimes there's a crust to dunk in it. Oh! How my mind wanders today. You must wonder what I'm going to gabble on about next. I can't help wondering what the mistress meant and why the master listened and went all quiet. What did she mean? Who is this body washer and what is he doing in a church?

Today, we went to the service as usual – the master and the mistress, and me a step behind them. Then there was Davey, who sleeps in the stables, keeping a short distance behind me. It's not too far along the track to Brookland, and I was content to be left to my own thoughts. Before long, we reached a trail of villagers meandering on their way to church, and a couple of maids from the bigger houses walked along either side of me. Mistress Ruth doesn't mind, as long as I show respect to my betters and don't chatter pointlessly. She needn't worry – I'm not the sort to say much. I would rather listen.

I mentioned the little church – the one sitting in the water at Fairfield. Ours is different altogether. I wouldn't call it grand, but it's long with aisles and extra chapels. Inside, the pillars lean outwards because the ground is soft, and buttresses stop them from tipping any further. Although the windows are plain glass, there is a patch of coloured that the old king's men forgot to smash out. Sometimes, after the service, I go to look at it and wonder what picture those colours were a part of. Towards the back, there's the font with all sorts of mouldings of men working and animals too. Once, when Mistress Ruth sent me to the market, I slipped into the church to have a proper look at those pictures. Our church doesn't have a stone tower; instead, there's a spire clad with wooden shingles and it's standing right there on the ground, rising as high as the church roof. People who have travelled to other places say they've never seen a spire like ours. I don't know if that's a good or a bad thing, and I don't like to ask because, perhaps, I am meant to know what they mean.

We stepped through the porch, then Mister Walter and Mistress Ruth settled midway down the nave, while Davey sat in the south aisle with his brothers and their families. I stood on my own, never sure of where to go, but knowing I must stay out of the way. The service went on and on, but I tried my best to listen and understand. All the words were in English, but not always the kind of English I understand. There were long words and clever words, but I kept my face turned towards the parson and he doesn't know if I say it right when we have to respond. If I move my lips when everyone else does, then no one can say I'm not being respectful to him and to God.

Today, the light shone through the plain glass windows and, where it rested on the whitewashed walls of the nave, I thought I could see the patterns and shapes from the paintings which have been covered up. I wondered if the whitewash would flake off and, in time, those old paintings would show through. Then I looked at the mistress and I saw she had her eye on me. I fixed my gaze on the parson and pretended that I had followed his every word. Later, when I say my prayers, I'll say sorry for wondering about those paintings and not listening as I should.

After the service, I was free to do as I wished, so I slipped between the belfry and the old stone walls of the church and looked up at my friend, the stone face. "How are you today?" I asked. "Have you seen anything interesting?" Then I continued, almost skipping through the churchyard and out to the back lane. For some time, I heard him telling me about the people he sees going about their business on the High Street. He reveals their secrets, and I confide mine. I told him about the row between the master and the mistress. He went quiet then because he couldn't explain what it was all about. It didn't matter; I was just pleased to be able to share my news and listen to his. By the time we had finished, I'd walked quite a way along Midley Wall road.

I know he was still back there on the church, but once I've started talking to him then I feel he is with me. Sometimes it seems like he is my only friend.

The lanes to Wheelsgate were narrow, the verges lush. I wore my best shawl and sturdy boots, but no cloak. The cloudless sky cheered me because rain over the past two Sundays had prevented me from going to see Kitty. I passed a few cottages between Brookland and Wheelsgate, half of them deserted. It's lonely, this place known as Walland Marsh.

I never feel alone for long because my sister does her best to come and meet me. By the time the house and barns of Wheelsgate were in sight, Kitty was marching out along the lane towards me. We both waved wildly, and I lengthened my stride.

"There you are!" she called. "I looked out for you these last two weeks. But I didn't think you'd come. Not with all the rain."

"I couldn't. Mistress Ruth would have scolded me if I'd got a soaking," I answered. "You know that."

"Are you hungry, Lucy?"

"Of course I am!" I grinned.

"There's a bit of bread and mutton left."

"That's good of your mistress." I usually arrived at Wheelsgate after they had eaten midday dinner and, if I was lucky, there might be some leftovers. "Got any news, Kitty?" I asked, as we approached the entrance to the farm.

"Not really," she responded. "Those two lambs we kept in the kitchen are out in the fields now. They were put out a day or two after you were last here. Oh! At church today the rector was late and smelt like he'd been at the brandy."

"Perhaps he was feeling ill," I suggested, not wanting to think bad of him, especially as he employed our older sister as a maid. "Perhaps he'd had a shock."

"He smells like it every week," she elaborated. "But he's not usually late."

"But did he give a good sermon?"

Kitty shrugged. "I wasn't really listening."

"And did you see Mary?" I asked.

"I did see her, but we didn't speak. I expect she was embarrassed by him smelling of the brandy. Mary must have been thinking that if she looked after him better, he wouldn't be needing the drink."

I said nothing and tried not to show my disapproval of Kitty and her sharp tongue. By now we were approaching the farmhouse and, although I visited every Sunday the weather allowed, I always felt a bit shy as I rounded the corner and went in through the kitchen door.

The farm is a lot bigger than the one I live in, with huge beams and some parts being rebuilt in red brick. Kitty says there are three rooms upstairs, while downstairs the mistress has her own parlour. Whereas I sleep on the kitchen floor, my sister has her own small room off the kitchen. At Deanes Farm, Davey sleeps in the stable loft; at Wheelsgate, there are a couple of men living in the barn loft and some small cottages for farm workers who have families.

"Sit yourself down," Kitty said, as we stepped into the warm kitchen. "I'll get the milk. I've never known someone as hungry as you." She always said that, and it always annoyed me because I missed my dinner to come and see her.

While I dipped crusts in the warm milk and chewed on strips of mutton, Kitty gossiped about the people she had seen at church that morning. I never failed to feel amazed about the things she learned and how bold she was to be chatting to people.

"You haven't asked me about Jack," she complained while I wiped a crust around the inside of my mug.

"I didn't know I was meant to."

Kitty raised her eyes to heaven, or the kitchen ceiling if I'm going to be exact. "Of course you were meant to. If you had a young man, then I'd be asking, wouldn't I?"

A young man! "Where would I find a man? I don't know what Mistress Ruth would say. I'd feel her shoe on my backside, that's for sure."

"You still haven't asked."

"Sorry Kitty." I pushed the mug aside and put my forearms on the scrubbed tabletop. "Did he speak to you, this Jack? Was he looking fine?"

"He didn't actually speak, but he kept turning back and looking." Her brown eyes went all dreamy. "Aye, he's changed the cuffs on his coat and trimmed his hair."

I sat upright. "He did all that for you! He must like you, Kitty."

"I'll say he does!" She smirked, then glanced towards the scullery. "We need to do the dishes."

"All right." The arrangement at Wheelsgate was that I could call in to see Kitty on a Sunday afternoon, but she still had to wash up after Sunday dinner. I swung my legs over the bench, but before we reached the scullery something popped into my curious mind. "A few months ago, they started tiling the floor. They've done this bit here and some over there, but why haven't they done any more?"

"They've run out of tiles, and the mistress is making a right fuss over it."

"Can't they get any more?"

"That's the problem – the master took them from the church out at Midley and now he won't go there or send any of his men."

"Why not?" I asked, a thrill running though me because I already knew the answer.

"Because the body washer lives there. Right there in the church."

That was the second time I'd heard of the body washer.

Lucy

I'd barely got the fire going when the master and the mistress started bickering early this morning. Their words started as a low mumble and, before long, their voices rose as he snapped and she could be heard taunting him. With them in the room above, and boards serving as both kitchen ceiling and bedroom floor, every word filtered down to me.

"I thought they were special to you," Mistress Ruth whined. "Saving them for the archbishop, you were."

"That's my business," Mister Walter snarled. "I've changed my mind, haven't I?"

"And you think someone will buy that old stuff?"

Heavy footsteps sounded on the floor above and dust scattered down onto the kitchen table. I sighed and reached for a cloth.

"Metal can be melted and made into something new, so I'm sure I'll find someone to part with a few shillings."

"And the box?" she queried. "Did you check to see if it had any pennies in it?"

"Oh! Interested now, are you? Wanting to take money from Midley?" He strode across the room and down the stairs.

"I was just asking," she screeched.

"It's a pretty thing. Carved by someone from Canterbury, or so they say. I'll keep it."

By the time he opened the door at the bottom of the stairs, I was on my knees sweeping the brick hearth and pretending I hadn't heard a word. Mister Walter took no notice of me. As he stepped into the kitchen, he turned back and shouted upwards, "I'm off to Tenterden. I'll see to the sheep out at Fairfield on the way. You can check the near fields or send the girl."

The master glanced at me then, and I gave a slight nod as I did every morning. I emptied the pan of ash into a bucket, hung the brush and pan on their nails by the fireplace and reached for the jar of oats. One... two... three scoops into the pan of milk.

Mistress Ruth clattered down the stairs. "I thought you weren't going to go touching those things." She lowered her voice, giving a menacing tone to her words: "You know why."

"I'll just tip them into a sack," he told her. "No harm in that."

The mistress looked at me then; I gave her a nod and turned back to the porridge.

"And there's no need for the girl to clean them if you're thinking of them going for melting?"

"No need," he agreed. "I'll go and bring the horse in, put the metal in a sack, then I'll be off." Mister Walter opened the door, looked back, and said, "I'll need something to eat."

He left the door swinging open. The day was warm, and the fire smoking, so I was glad of the fresh air.

"Slice some of yesterday's bread for the master and wrap it up with some cheese and a small jar of pickled vegetables," Mistress Ruth ordered.

"Now?" I asked. "The porridge..."

"Take the porridge off the heat. It will still thicken."

I retreated to the larder, snatching at the bread and cheese before the door closed on me.

The day passed peacefully. The mistress sent me to check over the sheep in the near fields with orders that I was to call Davey if I saw anything amiss. I wandered from field to field, crossing the waterways by plank bridges, sometimes stopping to peer down to watch the eels. At the water's edge, the reeds spouted their spring growth, and the long seedheads on the bulrushes were beginning to turn from green to brown. In the distance I could see the tiny church at Fairfield surrounded by wetland.

Everything appeared to be in order, with the ewes attending their lambs. On the way back, I passed Davey mending a bridge.

"How do the sheep fare, Miss Lucy?" he asked.

We don't speak much, but he's the only one here who calls me by my name. "They look fine," I answered. Then I stood for a moment, feeling awkward, shifting from foot to foot.

Davey put down his mallet and rose to his full height – which was several inches taller than Master Walter. He gave a slow smile and replied, "That's good." Then, as I began to walk away, "I'll be seeing you at dinner time."

"Aye. It will be a cold one. Mistress Ruth wants us to finish washing the undergarments today and give our Sunday clothes a good brushing. Shall I fetch yours?"

"You know where to find them..."

"I do."

Back in the yard, the mistress had already tipped the urine out of the huge pail lined with animal skin. The undergarments had been soaking in it since the previous morning, and now the shifts, chemises and hose lay in water and lye soap. The mistress had four shifts and I had three; it was the same with the men and their chemises, with the master having more than Davey.

"Here you go," Mistress Ruth said, handing me a stout pole. "Give 'em a prod."

Glad to have avoided the task of removing the garments from the urine, I took off my shawl and set about agitating the water, pushing the linens from side to side. "Time for a good soak now," I muttered after a while.

The mistress appeared with a basket containing the master's Sunday clothes. "Fetch Davey's breeches and jacket," she ordered, placing the basket on a bench and retrieving a couple of brushes from her apron pocket. "We'll give them a brush, and I noticed his cuffs need replacing. You can do them this evening, while I mend the hem on my skirt."

Wiping my hands on my apron, I walked across to the stables. The beasts were out to grass over the summer, and the stable floor was swept clean. Harnesses and halters hung from iron hooks. A soft light shone on layers of dust, and I found the place peaceful with the lingering scents of horses and their feed. A ladder took me to the loft and there, beyond the piles of last year's hay and separated by a plank wall, was Davey's place. It was small and the roof sloped, but I couldn't help envying him this space away from the master and the mistress and their constant bickering. Taking his best breeches and jacket from pegs on the plank wall, I retreated.

Like the master, who must have reached Tenterden by then, we ate a simple meal of Saturday's bread, cheese and pickled vegetables. Then Davey drew several buckets of water from the well, as Mistress Ruth and I set about the long process of rinsing the shifts, chemises and hose over and over. We worked in just our linens, with the heat of the day drying both our sweat and the inevitable splashes. Then we squeezed water from the undergarments as best we could and lay them on the grass behind the house where they could take advantage of the sunlight.

"I've put out the vegetables for the broth," Mistress Ruth said, as we paused to look with satisfaction at the clean linen and wool. "I'm off to check on the sheep."

"I'll start it now."

In the gloom of the kitchen, I chopped onions, turnips, skirret and carrots, adding them one by one to the pot to sizzle in a generous pool of melted lard. Then I grabbed fresh herbs from the garden and a scoop of barley from the larder. Pouring a jug of water into the pot, I left it all to simmer.

Throughout the afternoon, I shook and turned the linen and wool, while keeping an eye on the broth. The mistress returned, glanced towards the cooking pot and said, "Take the scraps out to the pigs."

I had my back to her so allowed myself the pleasure of scowling at her comment. For the past four years I had taken the scraps out – I didn't need telling.

As I headed through the doorway, Mistress Ruth called, "The master's on his way back. I saw him on his horse." Trailing after me, she continued, "I'd better get the eggs. I don't know how he expects us to manage when he goes off like that, leaving me with you and that useless, lumbering fool."

I didn't answer, and she wouldn't have expected me to, but I grimaced at her cruel words. Davey wasn't useless. He worked hard and without complaint. He knew the land and Mister Walter was lucky to have him.

Mistress Ruth and I were still outside when the master rode up and slid off the horse in an ungainly manner, letting the reins go, but placing a hand on the beast as if to steady himself. A sheen of sweat covered his face and neck, while his eyes glazed over. "Fetch me some ale," he ordered, his voice weak. "And get Davey to deal with the horse."

I glanced at the mistress and saw the look of horror on her face. She looked back at me. "Do as he says," she barked. Before I had reached the house, she called her next order: "Get the bottle of Four Thieves and put some on yourself."

I ran inside, my heart pounding. *Four Thieves! We've never used it before. Never had the need to. What does she mean? What am I to do first? He asked for ale, but she says to use the vinegar.* Through the kitchen I raced. *What am I to do first? I think she means for me to use the Four Thieves and then take the ale to him.*

With this settled in my mind, I rushed into the larder, thinking nothing of being shut inside, and snatched at the heavy jug of ale. Back into the kitchen I went and hastily poured some into a beaker. Leaving both jug and beaker on the table, I returned to the larder. *There it is. Up high.* Stretching, I reached for the flagon of vinegar infused with garlic, herbs and spices. *The Four Thieves. A bowl. I need a bowl.* Once more in the kitchen, I grabbed a bowl from the dresser and poured some of the precious liquid in it. *I don't want to die* – the thought flashed into my head. So, I picked up a clean rag and dipped it into the vinegar. With no thought as to how much I splashed, I wiped my face and neck, then dipped the cloth again and spread the pungent liquid over my forearms before rinsing my hands in the bowl.

By then the master and mistress were coming into the kitchen, he weaving about, seemingly unable to set one foot in front of the other.

"Drink it!" she shrieked, putting the ale to his mouth.

He made no effort to help himself, and so it was part drunk, part spilt down him and onto the earth floor. The mistress snatched at a cloth to clean him up and, as she pushed his chemise to one side, she wailed, "There's a boil! God save us – he's got a boil!"

The rush. The screaming. It was all too much for me. *What does she want of me now?* My arms and legs turned stiff, and it felt like an effort to move them.

Mistress Ruth gave me no time to think about what to do next. While she pulled off his jerkin and threw it on the floor, she babbled, "I'll get him up to bed. You must purify the air – here and in the bedroom."

I glanced at the Four Thieves, and she followed my gaze. Pushing the master towards the stairs, she ordered, "Get yourself up there, Walter. If you can't, we'll have to get Davey to help. I'm not strong enough." Then she took the cloth and wiped her face, forearms and hands with the infusion. Having done this, she turned her attention to me again: "The herbs. Get on with it, girl."

Herbs. I must cleanse the air.

Stumbling, I moved to the door. As I stepped outside, I turned back to see the master crawling up the stairs.

In the sunlight, I stood for a moment, eyes closed, breathing deeply. I became aware of the horse nearby. *He needs the saddle and bridle removed. But I am meant to be collecting herbs.* I faltered, unsure of what should be done next.

Fortunately, Davey sauntered into the yard. I looked at him and he looked back, as if he already knew something was wrong. At first, I felt that I had lost the power to speak, but somehow managed: "It's the master. He's ill. There's a boil."

"Is it…?" he asked, his voice gruff.

"Aye." I glanced towards the horse. "Can you put him in the field? Mistress Ruth wants me to burn herbs. There's Four Thieves in a bowl... in the kitchen."

I think Davey understood. "Take care of yourself, Lucy," he said. "Don't offer to nurse him. Maybe you'll be safe then."

I shrugged and turned away in the direction of the herb garden. If the mistress asked me to nurse him, then that's what I would do. It wasn't up to the likes of me to be picking and choosing what work I did.

Davey called after me, "Lucy, you need dried not fresh if it's to burn."

Turning once more, I went back to the house. The herbs lay in tied bunches on a wooden platter in the larder. *What was I thinking of, going to pick fresh ones?* Back in the kitchen, I took the rosemary and thyme by the stems and held a candle against the leaves until they smouldered. With a tray in the other hand, I began a slow walk around the kitchen table, wafting the herbs as best I could and ensuring ash fell into the tray.

When the air smelt pungent with the savoury smoke, I looked towards the open doorway and the stairs rising to the bedroom. A heaviness cloaked my body while I lifted one foot, then the next, and up I went towards the plague room.

I've said it now: plague.

Davey

At first light, I went to the open door of the farmhouse and peered in. Lucy stood at the kitchen table, her hands in a deep bowl, kneading dough.

"You've started early," I commented.

She shrugged. "I have to do something."

"The mistress is lucky to have you." I feel sorry for Lucy and do my best to offer a kind word here and there. The master and the mistress do not treat her cruelly, but they are sharp with her and think nothing of serving a quick slap. The pair of them thrive on their constant bickering, and poor Lucy must suffer from living amongst all the scolding and snapping.

"I'm lucky to have good food in my belly and a warm bed to sleep in," she replied.

I have my place in the stable loft, the warmth from the horses over the winter months, and many peaceful hours in my own company. My brothers live in Brookland, not far along the lane, and sometimes I join them for a drop of ale in the tavern. When I compare my life to Lucy's, I know I am the lucky one.

"How is he?"

"The mistress says I should go for the curate." I nodded my understanding, and she continued, "His breaths are shallow, and I can see the boils from the doorway. The mistress tries to cool him with rose scented water, but there is nothing to be done to ease his discomfort."

"I wonder if the curate will come?" I said, partly to myself.

"He could pray from the church?" she answered, her tone uncertain.

"You're right. That's probably what he will do."

Lucy smiled. I bet Mistress Ruth has never told her she was right about anything.

"When are you going to the village?" I asked.

"Soon," she replied. "I'll cover this and leave it to rise in the sunshine." Lucy turned the dough over and reached for a cloth. "It's not too early, is it? Too early for the curate?"

I considered this for a moment. "Nay. Not by the time you've got yourself ready and walked there."

Lucy passed me with the bowl of dough. "There's no need for you to go in there, Davey," she said, jerking her head in the direction of the farmhouse. "Stay in your loft and out on the land. I know I should feed you but…"

"I'll see to myself," I told her. "Stay well, Lucy."

It was the most I had ever spoken to her. She's a sweet girl.

I busied myself on the 'home' fields – my own word for the land close to the farmhouse, the stables and barns. Most of the land there has never seen the plough, instead we breed stocky Romney sheep. They are tough beasts who tolerate the Marsh winds and lack of shelter. Like us, they navigate the winding drainage ditches and boggy areas. The Romney's wool is prized as being both long and fine; it fetches a good price at market and even more when smuggled from our beaches and across the Channel. Not that I should speak of these things – we must never speak of it.

The skies above Romney Marsh were a clear blue, the clouds sparse and high. Wind blew briskly, bringing with it a chill which nipped at my arms. Perhaps I should have worn a jacket rather than a jerkin, but I soon warmed through once I was striding across fields and over plank bridges. I checked the lambs were accounted for and safely with their mothers, and that both ewes and infants looked to be in good health. Then I returned to the land nearest the farm and, having fetched a hoe, I set about the task of keeping the vegetable plots in good order. Now expecting Lucy to reappear at any time, I kept an eye out and strolled across to meet her in the lane.

"He won't come but says the mistress can recite the prayers for the dying. When… if… I'm to tell him and he'll send word to the…" Lucy paused, and she looked at me, her eyes wide and her mouth opening and closing although no words were uttered.

"The?"

"The body washer... him who washes them after..."

I nodded my understanding.

We glanced towards the farmhouse and up to the bedroom window with its wide-open shutters. As we did so a long, lingering wail drifted towards us. I looked at Lucy and she looked at me. Then she turned and trudged towards the house. She's always been an anxious little thing, but today she appears more cowed than ever.

Lucy

In the farmhouse, as I sweep, scour and fan the smouldering rosemary and thyme about the place, I keep as quiet as possible. It's best that I don't bother Mistress Ruth with my noise or chatter. Best that I put a meal in front of her and keep the place clean but keep my thoughts to myself. In the yard, there's a pile of ashes from the master's bedding. We don't talk about him and what happened.

The mistress said we mustn't go to church, that people wouldn't want us there, even if we used Four Thieves beforehand. But I went and sat on the grass outside, in the space between the wooden belfry and the stone church, and I chatted quietly to my friend.

"Mister Walter has gone," I told the stone face. "It was the plague." He said he was very sorry to hear that, and he hoped I was keeping the air pure at home. Then he asked how I was feeling, and I thought that was kind of him because no one ever asks how I am. After a while, I told him that I was going to see Kitty, and he didn't have anything to say about that. I said my goodbyes and off I went.

As I left Brookland behind me and spotted the rooftops of Wheelsgate Farm, my spirits lifted. I straightened my back and held my head a little higher. At times I felt myself smiling as I watched lambs gambolling and spotted the bright turquoise bodies of dragonflies darting over the water. When I saw Kitty walking towards me, I waved madly and felt a grin spill across my whole face. Kitty didn't wave back, and I thought nothing of it until we neared, and she put her palm out before her.

"Keep back!" she shouted.

I stood stock still, the smile wiped from my face, my body slumping.

"You can't come to Wheelsgate today, Lucy. You might have the plague. You'll pass it on to us."

Tears welled immediately. How foolish I had been. How stupid to think I could go to see Kitty.

"I had to come and check, just in case..." Kitty continued, "but I thought you would know."

"Mistress Ruth didn't say..." I began, but then I remembered I hadn't told her my plans.

"No one wants you here," Kitty stated. How could my own sister be so cruel?

"When can I come?"

"I don't know." Kitty turned away and took a few steps, then she paused and looked back at me. "I hope you don't get it, Lucy. I hope you stay well."

"Thank you," I muttered, but she had her back to me.

I hadn't wept for Mister Walter or in fear of me getting the plague, but now the tears poured down my face, my nose ran, and I gulped noisily while trying to breathe. Time passed and I began to calm down, then a plan began to form in my mind. Having lifted my skirt to wipe my face, I set off along the track we call Midley Wall.

The track rose higher than the land, its being an old seawall. The sea that had retreated couldn't be seen from the top of it, but everyone knew that if the winds and the tide were strong enough then it could break through the distant earth banks and come spilling inland. Maybe the sea would reach Midley Wall. Then the men would have to start again with draining the land and rebuilding the walls.

Before long, I dropped down from the raised track and trailed along the edge of a waterway, slowing as I drew closer to Midley church. Then I sat on a tussock of dry grass, facing the southern side. Although I wasn't close enough to see every detail, the church appeared to be in a forlorn state, as Mister Walter had told us. Its walls were an odd mixture of brick and stone, the small nave windows open to the weather and crumbling away at the edges. No wooden shingles remained on the spire, while I could see a couple of gaping holes in the main roof.

I stood and, still separated by the water, edged my way towards the east end. A sense of doubt settled upon me. *What am I doing here?* I asked myself. *Well, you've got to do something, and Kitty doesn't want you.* I scowled at the unfairness of being unwelcome at Wheelsgate. Once I drew level with the chancel end, I paused. The decorative window was empty of glass, although the pillars still rose high to a point. I'd have liked to peep through the window, but I had stayed the far side of a waterway and couldn't see a bridge nearby.

I'll just sit here and watch for a while. Weary from the troubles at home over the past week and fearful of who the plague would touch next, I found the warmth of the sun soothing. Midley seemed deserted. My eyes closed, I slumped to the ground, and my breathing deepened until I fell into a heavy sleep.

Waking with a jolt, I felt my forehead throbbing. I sat, ashamed of my wasting time sleeping, and allowed the headache to subside. A slight movement by the chancel alerted me to the fact that I was no longer alone, and a flush rose from my neck to my cheeks. Standing with his back to the church, a man gazed directly at me. With the church on a slight rise, and me still sitting, I looked back. *What's he doing staring at me? I wish he wouldn't.*

Frowning, I studied his fair hair, clear skin, and long, slim body. *Who is he? Some lad from one of the farms?*

He turned and walked around the far side of the church so I could no longer see him. I pulled myself to my feet. *I'd better get back home. God help me if the mistress is in a bad mood.*

As I followed the waterway, the tower end of the church came into view again and now someone else appeared. A woman scurried along, bent over a basket, a light shawl covering her head and upper body. On reaching the tower, which doubled as a porch, she placed several packages on a small table, turned and left. Not once did she look about the place, so she didn't see me and, presumably, she didn't see the man.

Curious to see what happened next, I paused. The young man appeared from the far side of the church, picked up the packages and took them inside.

I headed off, conscious of Mistress Ruth and her fury at my being so late. Back to the raised track, Midley Wall, I went, and all the time my thoughts raced: *Could it be him? Could he be the body washer? He must be. I didn't think… I didn't expect him to be young.*

By the time I was walking the track to Brookland, I was wondering if the body washer would be calling at my home again soon.

Lucy

I am exhausted. My eyes smart from the smoke rising from herbs smouldering in clay dishes and feel as dry as old bones. I can taste the burning rosemary and thyme and wonder if I could ever tolerate them in my food again. My skin reeks of vinegar and garlic – the main ingredients included in the Four Thieves which I wipe over my body several times a day – and my fingertips smell of the onion I rub on Mistress Ruth's boils.

The plague did not stop with the master. But where his suffering lasted no more than a night and a morning, hers has lingered over three days. For all my complaints about how tired and weak I feel, I have not been touched by the Black Death.

I have not been touched by it yet.

Day and night, I soothe the mistress' burning skin with warm water scented with essence of lavender and rose. I turn her sheets about on the bed, so she lies on a dry patch, then lift her the best I can and change her nightshift for a fresh one. Through the darkest hours, I doze fitfully on an upright chair and only leave her to frantically rinse and wring the shifts, then put them out to dry. Porridge is my only sustenance, having no time for peeling and chopping vegetables, but it suits me well. Davey fends for himself, while leaving milk on the doorstep for me.

Mistress Ruth does not complain as I would have expected. Instead, she accepts my care. If she were to whine and wail as normal, then I would know that the mistress had some fight in her, but I know she is ready to submit to the plague. Perhaps it will be tonight when she passes from this earth. Perhaps it will be tomorrow.

When it is my turn, I wonder if I will be ready to surrender or if I will find the strength to rail against almost certain death.

Avery

Today I met the girl. She didn't speak to me. I wonder if she *can* speak, but I suspect she is so fearful and so depleted that she cannot find the energy.

On entering the open doorway of the farmhouse, I thought the kitchen was empty of people. Then I noticed her squatting on the edge of a pallet in the shadows of the staircase. She looked up at me, her face blank, then jerked her head upwards to indicate where the dead woman lay.

A pan of water hung over a meagre fire. I tipped some into the large jug I carried in my basket. The girl watched me and then she stood and walked slowly, as if her whole being ached, towards the hearth. She crouched, picked up a log, and lay it gently amongst the bones of the fire.

I moved towards the stairway, the basket in the crook of my arm and the jug cradled in both hands. Once upstairs, I faced the body of a woman on the bed and offered a quick prayer, "Lord, take this woman into your loving arms and free her from the pain and misery she has suffered on this earth. Help me tend her with the love and respect that your son taught us. Amen." I placed the basket on the floor, withdrew a shallow bowl and, having put it on a small table, poured the water into it. Next, I took scent and soft rags from the basket. Before I began the tender task of cleansing Ruth's body, I noticed a clean shift hanging over the back of a chair and silently thanked the girl.

When I had finished, I stepped towards the open window and took in the view of flat fields, reed-lined waterways and sheep. I closed my eyes and breathed deeply. Then turned back to the bed, gave a last nod of respect to the dead woman and left.

At the doorway to the farmhouse, I met the men who were about to collect the body and take it to the plague pits at Old Romney.

"She's ready for you," I said. They merely nodded their response.

I didn't see the girl again. Maybe she was still sitting in the kitchen. Maybe she had gone outside.

When I settle on my mattress within the church at Midley, I will pray that I won't be back to tend to her young body.

Lucy

A month has passed since the mistress died. The Black Death wrapped itself around me, yet I am still here. In those first dark days, I burned everything that could have harboured the plague, including my own mattress and the rugs. Then, starting in their bedroom, I washed and scrubbed every surface. I had little else to do – no mistress to please, no one else to feed or look after.

Davey cares for himself now. Morning and evening, he milks the two cows we keep for our own use, throwing much of the milk away. Then he goes out to check on the looker in the far fields and the sheep in the home fields. My world is small – just the house, the yard and the vegetable plots. I see him several times nearby, and he raises his hand as a greeting.

It seems that, this time, both Davey and I have been spared. I have no news to share of other people and other places. Until today, I hadn't even been as far as Brookland village since the mistress became ill.

I hate sleeping alone in the farmhouse. In the blackest hours of the night, I find myself missing the rumble of the master's snores and the occasional whine of complaint from the mistress. Last night an idea came into my mind and, foolish as it seemed, I couldn't shake it off.

"I'll do it," I voiced my thoughts aloud, having risen from my bed in the early hours, opened the shutters and prodded the fire into life.

By the time I had cut thick slices of bread and a chunk of cheese, and carefully poured weak ale into a clay flask, my porridge was bubbling. I ate from the pan, as quickly as I could without burning my mouth, then left it empty on the table. *There's no one to nag at me now*, I thought, as I packed a small wicker basket and opened the door. On the threshold, my gaze darted about as I scanned the yard for a sign that Davey was nearby. *He's probably out in the fields.* With this, I scampered to the lane and from there I walked on and on along the straight lane called King Street towards Brenzett, thinking it would make a change from taking the route through Brookland. It did make a difference, but it was a dull sort of road, nothing but the track, with a drainage ditch on each side and then acres of pasture. Every so often I passed a cottage but kept my gaze fixed straight ahead, not wanting to start a conversation with anyone or see them back away from me, unsure if I had been spared from the plague.

I felt glad to reach Brenzett and began to relax. *They won't know me here,* I thought. *I'm just a maid passing through.* Ambling along, I looked at stalls set up outside cottages, seeing what the villagers had to sell. It was a quiet place, but I passed a lad with a barrow and another with a cart, and women carrying baskets and hurrying children along. I didn't linger, not having spoken to anyone much in a whole month and not knowing these Brenzett folk. I didn't want to find myself stuck for how to reply, or having to say who I was and what reason I had for passing by.

On reaching a crossroads, I turned right, leaving the village behind me. Now I walked atop a wide bank known as the Rhee. I liked it being high, looking down on the land either side. Occasionally I passed a cottage perched up there, away from the lower ground, and I thought to myself that the people in those homes would be glad to be above the marshy land during the winter months. The Rhee led directly to Old Romney, so I could walk along, lost in my thoughts, and with no need to consider if I was on the right path or track. Once in Old Romney, I felt drawn to the church, not having been to mine in Brookland since the master fell ill.

Passing by cottages and barns, a woman carrying a basket of eggs, a boy holding a cat under his arm, and a group leading a horse and cart laden with hay, I approached St Clement's church. Once in the churchyard, I paused to gaze up at it. I shouldn't think badly of a holy building, but privately I thought it to be a dumpy place, held up by huge buttresses. It was not as large or impressive as Brookland, but it did sit on a rise, and I liked the way the tower rested snug against the south-western corner.

Once inside, I sat hunched in prayer, breathing in the scents of damp stone and wood combined with the sweetness of roses in vases. The sun shone through the chancel window, bringing the altar cloth and cross to life, diminishing the light from the two candles. Neither the sunlight nor its warmth reached me, and I left, having prayed for the master and mistress and given thanks that I had been spared.

"I thought it was you, Lucy!" A merry voice shook me from my thoughts as I stepped from the gloom of the porch to be bathed in the heat of the sun.

"Oh! Mary!" A huge grin spilt across my face. "I've just arrived. I was going to come to the back and see if..." The words trailed away because, however pleased I was to see my sister, she wasn't the reason for me coming to Old Romney.

"Kitty said... She said... Lucy, we thought you were dead. That you had... You know..."

"I'm not dead," I stated. "I never was. But Mister Walter is and Mistress Ruth too."

Mary, older than me by four years, studied me carefully. "But you're well? It's here, you know. There's been six of our people put in the pit, not in the churchyard."

"I'm well. And you? Are you in good health?"

"Aye, I'm fine and as happy as anything to see you."

"I'm sorry I never get to see you, Mary," I began as we walked out of the churchyard. "Mistress Ruth only let me off work on a Sunday and that's your busy day looking after the rector and his wife." I glanced towards the rectory.

"It's just him now," Mary informed me. "She's gone." My sister looked up to the heavens. "The rector won't mind if you come in for a chat. He's off visiting anyway."

I was keen to spend time with Mary, who was never as bossy as Kitty, but I had come to Old Romney for another reason, so I hesitated while considering my reply. "I will, Mary. Thank you. But not yet, I've got something to do. So, if you don't mind, I'll be back in no time." Without waiting for an answer, I started walking down the track, then turned and called, "I'll come to your kitchen door. Won't be long."

Back to the road I went, past the beautiful red brick Manor House, and took the ancient lane which would eventually lead to New Romney. I passed farm workers' cottages, and then the ruins of St Lawrence's Church, and put the village behind me. Before long, a well-trodden track turned off the lane. I took a few steps along it and paused. "You're close enough, Lucy," I murmured. "Close enough to see it. Far enough to keep safe."

Other than the sheep cropping the grass, there was no one else about. I edged closer. "That's enough. Say your prayers and go back to Mary."

I took a few steps closer, just enough so I could see the shape and size of the pit, not close enough to see the layer of fresh earth and lime I heard they put over the bodies. I would have liked to see how deep it was and to work out how many more it would take. "You've been spared. Keep away," I muttered. "You've seen enough."

I stepped back, bowed my head and prayed. "Dear Lord in heaven, please treat Mister Walter and Mistress Ruth kindly and forgive them their sharp tongues. They went to church every Sunday, so please give them your blessing. Thank you, God, for sparing me. I'll try to be good and will go back to church now a month has passed. I didn't go before but I still said my prayers. Amen."

Rhythmic footsteps could be heard in the direction of New Romney, and I saw two sets of men, each carrying a bier with a covered body. "There's more coming. Best be off." I glanced in the direction of the plague pit. "Sorry I said about your sharp tongues. You were only trying to teach me right from wrong." Then I turned and scurried back to see Mary, my curiosity satisfied.

Davey

We can't carry on like this, me living in the barn loft and Lucy in the house. I've got the sheep and the land to tend to, but she is lost without the master and mistress to cook and clean for. She's been busy, I won't say otherwise, but she has no purpose to her life now. Lucy is a young woman who likes to keep occupied and please others. Things need to change around here. We have been spared the plague, thank the Lord, and must think to our future.

The master and the mistress were not the only ones to suffer. We have lost our looker who tended the sheep out towards Fairfield. I found him dead in the hut one morning and can only be thankful that his passing was quick. He and his family lived in a one-room cottage perched on high ground that once served as an embankment to keep the sea out. There were three grown sons and a daughter and, when I went to tell them about our good looker, I met the daughter of the family drawing water from the well.

"Don't come any closer, Davey," she called. "Ma and two of my brothers have the fever. Robert is out lookering towards Appledore and Pa is tending yours."

I passed on my terrible news the best I could from a distance.

"I hoped he might be spared," she said, her tone weary. "He's not home much in the springtime, although he did complain of a headache when we last saw him. Sunday, I think it was."

We spoke a little more, me telling her how the master had often praised her father for being such a hard worker and how much he was valued. None of it was the truth – Mister Walter only complained, and I never heard him sound pleased about anything or anyone. She looked too tired to absorb the news, let alone hold a conversation, and said, "Davey, I best get back inside. There's three of them to care for as well as I can, and no rest for me."

I had my work to get on with – more than ever with the looker gone. A week passed and I decided to go to the cottage and see how they fared. No smoke rose from the chimney, the door and shutters were all open, and I saw no movement.

"They've all gone."

I jumped, not realising that an old man had crept up behind me.

"That's awful news," I murmured to myself. He had passed by, apparently with nothing else to say.

That was two, perhaps three, weeks ago. So, you can imagine my surprise when a lad approached me while I was checking on the sheep this morning. I watched him and, as soon as he neared me, I put up my hand.

"Stay back," I called. "You're sickening for something?" His face was pale, while large blotches marked his neck, face and forearms.

"I won't come any closer, but the plague has passed through me. I bear the scars and I'm the only one left from my family, but I'm getting stronger every day."

"You look familiar."

"Aye, my father was your looker on the land towards Fairfield."

I grinned and my body felt lighter than it had in weeks. "I heard you had all gone! It's good to see you."

"It's good to see a friendly face. I'm Robert."

"Davey."

"Who's in charge of this land now?" he asked.

Without pausing, I told him, "I am. There's no one else. Master Walter and Mistress Ruth had no children, you see. And we never saw any other family."

"So, you farm it now?"

"I do. The master always said that's how it would be when he was taken to a better place." I gazed upwards. *Please God, forgive me my untruths.*

"Would you give me work and a place to lie my head at night?"

"I'd do it gladly," I responded.

While Robert voiced his thanks, my head spun with ideas and plans. I needed a labourer, but also time to put my schemes into place.

"I've not moved into the farmhouse yet," I told him. "Lucy and I have been spared the plague, but the whole place needed cleaning. So much has been burnt and the rest of it washed. Come back in two days and there will be a bed for you in my loft – it's good and snug. You'll have work all year round and decent meals with us in the kitchen. How does that suit you?"

"It suits me well," Robert answered.

We were about to part ways when I thought to ask, "How old are you?"

"Seventeen years," he replied.

"A fine age." This lad was old enough to have some sense, strong enough to survive the plague, but young enough not to ask any questions about my elevation to farmer.

I strolled back to the farmhouse with a plan in mind. "Lucy!" I called at the open door. "It's been a month – time to make plans. Lucy... are you there?"

The kitchen was deserted. A pan encrusted with dry porridge sat on the table, logs smouldered on the hearth and her bed under the stairs had been left without her straightening the sheets and blanket. I opened the door to the staircase and walked up the steep stairs directly into the dusky bedroom. Heading towards the cracks of light, I pushed the shutters open. The room showed no signs of its previous occupants – a bedframe filled most of the space, bare of any mattress or curtains, and no clothes remained on pegs or thrown over the back of the one chair. The two trunks were open and empty, and the only ornament was a bowl of rose petals set on a small table.

I nodded my approval. The sloping ceilings may be low in places, and I would, no doubt, suffer for knocking my head on the beams, but it made an improvement on my space within the barn loft. From the window, I looked out towards the little church at Fairfield and then down to the late mistress' herb garden, but Lucy could not be seen.

Back downstairs, I peeped into the larder and noticed that a pan of congealed broth had been placed on a shelf. Lucy must have been gone for some time and had made no preparations for a hot midday meal. *She must be feeling lost without the master and mistress to serve. It's not right. Not right at all. She needs to feel useful.*

I was about to leave and look around the farmyard and home fields when Lucy bustled in, an empty basket tucked under her arm. Her brow creased as soon as she saw me and her mouth opened into a round 'o'.

"Here you are," I said, trying to keep my manner friendly. "I was wondering where you were."

"I was…" she started and then a blush began to spread from her neck upwards and she looked at the floor. But I never learnt where she had been, and she continued with, "Is it all right now? Is it all right for you to come in here? I've got no dinner ready, but I can make supper."

"I think we have been spared," I replied. "Now, Lucy, we need to talk about what we are going to do. Here we are, me and you, living here with no master and mistress. We need to do something about it."

"You mean leave?" she squeaked. "But where?"

"There's no need to leave. They had no sons, nor daughters either. I say that you and I take on the farm. How about it, Lucy? I'll be master and you'll be the mistress. As long as we pay the rent then it seems fair enough."

She looked straight at me, her eyes wide, her brow still creased. I could see that I hadn't explained myself very well, so I started again.

"We can run this place, can't we? I've seen Robert today; you know he used to do the lookering with his father…"

"But he's dead!" The words burst from her, and she made the sign of the cross on her chest.

"He's not! The rest of them are, but Robert is very much alive. He's going to live in the barn loft and work for me." I pulled out a chair and sat at the scrubbed table, hoping to put the poor girl at ease. She looked like a frightened rabbit, standing there before me.

"That's good," she replied, her voice calmer. "Good about Robert. He's going to live in the barn with you."

"Nay, I'll be in the house." I jerked my head upwards, indicating my intention to set up home in the house and make my bed in the room upstairs. "We can get married, Lucy. You and I. Then I'll be master, you'll be mistress, and we'll run this place. But we'll be kindly, not like they were. What do you think, Lucy? Shall we get married?"

"I'd never thought about being married," Lucy answered, her hands twisting the handle of the basket, so it circled slowly. "I didn't think the mistress would let me."

"How old are you?" I asked.

"Seventeen, I think."

"I'm twenty-three. Old enough to take care of you," I told her.

"I like you, Davey. You're always kind to me. I don't know anything much about being married, but I know how to cook and clean and wash the clothes."

"Maybe we'll get a girl to help you," I suggested. "Not yet. But later, if we need one." I paused, and Lucy said nothing in reply. Most likely she was considering the changes which would take place as soon as the banns had been read and the date arranged. "Well, I'll go and speak to the curate, and I think we can get back to normal now," I said. "I mean eating our meals together. I'll fix up a mattress for the bed upstairs. You take some coins from Mistress Ruth's pot and get some linen sheets hemmed by Goodwife Anne in the village. I think we can make do with our blankets, but we'll treat ourselves to more in the autumn.

"All right," she said, looking towards the larder door. "I'll add to yesterday's broth and get our supper on to cook. We'll have meat – and plenty of it. It's a celebration, isn't it?"

"It is!" I grinned. "We'll eat our supper here tonight as master and mistress of this house!"

I watched as a huge smile spread over Lucy's face. It reached her eyes, and she stopped looking so nervous.

"I'll be off to see the curate then, and we'll start going to church again. He'll want to ask us every Sunday for three weeks if it's what we want and if there is any reason why we can't marry."

"He will," she agreed. "And after that we'll marry."

I pictured my mother putting on a feast for us, and my brothers and their jesting, but I wasn't sure if Lucy had any family. She went somewhere on a Sunday, I thought, but where I couldn't say. "Do you have anyone you need to tell?" I asked. "Family?"

Lucy fell silent for a moment before responding, "Nay. There's just Kitty and she won't put herself out to come along to see me. And there's Mary at Old Romney..." She looked down at her hands, still grasping the basket, then her words came out in a rush. "I don't go over there, do I? I can't say when I last saw Mary. But when we're married, you'll be my family, won't you, Davey?"

"I will." Standing up, I walked up to her and briefly put my hand on hers. "I'll be off to Brookland then."

Mary

My master, rector of Old Romney and Midley, received a letter today. He read it standing in the study, where light from the front window fell upon the thick paper. I placed a tray with a beaker of wine and some spiced biscuits on his desk, as I always do if he is at home in the afternoon, then silently slipped back to the kitchen.

Since his wife died, he tends to share the news with me. I listen and murmur my agreement or express my sorrow, then go back to my chores. On my return, he was eager to talk.

"Ah! Mary, I have a letter from Canterbury – from one of the archbishop's men. The next visitation will include Old Romney, so I must prepare." He glanced at the letter again. "They will be here within the next couple of weeks."

"Here?" I squeaked. "How are we to…?" I had to suppress an urge to race along the lane to Goodwife Beth's cottage and tell her the news. Instead, I asked, "Do you think we will feed the archbishop? I'm sure Goodwife Beth will do her best, but there is only the small dining table to eat at."

"Nay, he'll be entertained in style at Lydd or New Romney and will merely pass through our small place."

I calmed down and listened, standing before him with my head slightly bowed and hands clasped before me.

"Archbishop Parker is visiting every church on Romney Marsh. He'll look at the condition of the building and its grounds, and check services are held regularly. Mary, what is to be done if he finds us lacking? We have but fifteen houses in the village and not enough money to care for the church."

I didn't reply. He didn't expect me to. I had opinions, but it was not my place to express them. *Sir, please wear your surplice when the archbishop comes. Please wear it every day, so that when he speaks to your parishioners none of them say that sometimes you preach in layman's clothes.*

"The roof above our Lady Chapel has not been repaired," Reverend Edward Kenelm continued. "If I have asked the roofer once, then I have asked a hundred times."

"He is not a Godly man," I ventured to comment, "but his wife is a good woman, and our mothers were close friends. Let me speak to her?"

"What would I do without you?"

I raised my gaze to see him beaming at me. Your wife has been gone these past six months, and your son with her. It is time to smile again. Time to remember to wear your surplice.

"I am just doing my job," I replied.

"Nay, Mary! Your job is to tend to the house. Not listen to my ramblings or assist me with my troubles. If my curate..." His words tailed away. Rather than being a young man who the rector could mould to his liking, the curate was, unusually, an older man who had come to the Church late in life. He had none of the zeal my Reverend Kenelm needed in his assistant.

"The curate is unwell," I reminded him. "I believe he caught a chill when he last went to Midley to take a service. He got drenched in rain on the walk back."

"A service no one attends."

"Barely a soul lives there," I reasoned. "Those who do, go to other churches." I paused, knowing I had said too much. "Or so my sister, Kitty, says. She's at Wheelsgate, you know. Close to Midley."

"Better they go to Lydd or Brookland than not at all," Reverend Kenelm declared. He considered his words for a moment. "They don't come here to St Clement's."

"Because those living in the parish are closer to the other churches." I had said enough.

"If our good curate has taken to his bed, then I must go to Midley next Sunday. Just in case..."

No one will be there, I thought. *Only the body washer and he makes himself scarce on a Sunday.*

"I will pray for the curate's good health," I told Reverend Kenelm, "and for the archbishop's goodwill towards us."

"What would I do without you?" he repeated.

"I must..." I picked up the tray containing an empty glass and a plate with one biscuit remaining. My mouth watered as I glanced towards the door.

"Of course. Thank you. God bless you, dear Mary."

Back in the kitchen, I stirred the mutton stew prepared by Goodwife Beth. She comes to the rectory six mornings a week to make a dinner for the rector and myself. Every other day, one of us bakes a loaf of bread. On Sunday, I cook our main meal. My other duties include tending the fires, laundering clothes, scouring, sweeping and dusting. I work on our vegetable plots, although the heavy labour is done by a lad who also chops the wood, draws water from the well, tends the chickens and any number of jobs that need doing to keep the rectory in good order.

When I speak of the meals shared with Reverend Kenelm, I don't mean it to sound as if we eat together. He sits at his small table in the parlour, and I am at the kitchen table. It can be a lonely life. I enjoy the time when Goodwife Beth is bustling about the place, but, all too soon, she is gone, and I'm left with my thoughts. People come and go, to see the rector. No one comes to see me.

Twice a week, I walk along the old lane which runs beside the Wallingham Sewer and takes me to New Romney. Now, there's a place full of life with shops lining the High Street, stalls showing their wares, and market traders calling for attention. Inns serve ale, wine and spirits while the people of the town serve the Lord in a magnificent church. Mills stand on mounds, and a shallow bay is home to a small fishing fleet. New Romney is a town that hums with busyness from dawn to dusk. I am eager to go there, to fill my basket with food for our larder, or to spend the pennies I collect in my purse on material, trimmings or scent. Afterwards, when I turn my back on the town, I am glad to return to our peaceful village.

At night I sleep in a small, windowless room off the kitchen. There is a low attic room, but Goodwife Beth says, and I agree, that it wouldn't be right for a young maid to be in the main part of the house with the widowed rector. So, while he is in his bedroom, both the nursery and attic stand empty, and I am in the lean-to. In the winter, I keep the door to the kitchen open so I can benefit from the heat radiating from the fire. In the summer, I can only hope a breeze might enter my stuffy space and I will wake feeling refreshed.

I wonder what will become of Lucy now both her master and mistress have passed from this life. I must speak to Goodwife Beth about her, and we can look out for a place for my sister here in Old Romney. Lucy is so willing to please that anyone would be lucky to have her come and work for them. In the meantime, I shall ask Reverend Kenelm if I can walk along to Brookland one afternoon and see if all is well there. Lucy needs someone to guide her, and I fear she will be feeling lost. When we spoke, she never did explain to me what is happening now at Deanes Farm. If Mister Walter and Mistress Ruth had a son, or a nephew, perhaps he will come and take charge of the place. I hope he is kind to my dear sister.

My thoughts wander. Until I go there for myself, I won't know how she fares and if she needs my help.

"It's me, Mary!" I called at the open door of a neat cottage on Five Vents Lane.

"Mary, Katherine's girl?" I heard movement and a slim woman with bright eyes appeared. "Aye, it is you."

"Not much of a girl now," I responded with a smile.

"You'll always be a girl to me, and here you are – working at the rectory. Your mother, God rest her soul, would be proud of you. Come and sit down on the bench with me. Tell me your news."

I followed Margery around to the back of her low cottage. "It's the rectory I've come about," I told her as we sat down, our backs to the wood-framed walls and thickly thatched roof. Before us were acres of sheep pasture and gently winding waterways, with barely another cottage in sight. I turned to glance up at the reed-thatch roof. "Well, church business really."

"He sent you, did he?" Margery's lips pulled in, showing her disapproval. "Six months it's been. Six months! Some men would have married and had another babe on the way by now. Not him. You need to have a word – tell him to wear his surplice, so we can all see he's a man of God, and to keep a closer eye on his parishioners. There are some who need a guiding hand."

"Me? I'm just…"

"Nay, Mary, you're not 'just'. Your father was a fine carpenter, employing two men, and your mother was related to the Wilcocks of Lydd and New Romney. She could read and write. Taught you three girls, she did. I don't know how Lucy took to it. Kitty is bright enough but lazy. You have a neat hand though, and I bet the rector knows it. Does he make use of it?"

I nodded slowly. "I wrote a letter for him when he felt low and couldn't find the right words. Sometimes he asks me to pass on a message – that's why I'm here today. There's going to be a visit from the archbishop himself. He wants to look at the church – this one here and Midley too. The rector is worried about the roof of the Lady Chapel."

"He'll be wanting my Jed to see to it," Margery stated. "I'll tell him when he gets home."

"He'll do it?"

"Of course. He's got a stack of slate over there in his store." She pointed towards an open barn. "It came from the old church, St Lawrence, and he's keeping it safe for whenever the rector needs it."

"Oh! He'll do it soon?"

"He'll be there tomorrow with his ladders and slate. Don't worry, Mary. I know how to handle my Jed."

I didn't know what to say to that, not after all those months of Reverend Kenelm fretting over the roof and nothing being done about it.

"How's your patchwork bedcover?" Margery asked.

"Coming along nicely, thank you." I beamed to think of my time spent stitching scraps of material together. "But it will have to be put aside once the nights draw in. If there's sewing to be done over the winter, it will be collars and cuffs, and then there's the darning."

"There's never enough hours in the day for a woman," Margery observed.

"I'd better get back," I replied, standing up. "I'll call by again when there's news to share. Thank you for telling Jed about the roof. The rector has all sorts to think of, what with the archbishop on his way."

"If it takes his mind off his loss and opens his eyes to how fortunate he is, it's no bad thing," Margery declared.

"I don't like to think disrespectfully about him," I replied with more confidence than I felt.

"You're a good girl, Mary," Margery called out as I left. "You, Kitty and Lucy were all sweet girls – but you're the most sensible of the lot. I've got high hopes for you."

Hopes for me! Whatever is she thinking about? Relieved about the roof repairs, I headed to the rectory.

Mary

Today I had time to myself while the rector called on some of the local families. I already had a needle and thread to hand, having turned and stitched the hem on his best surplice, and my thoughts moved to my patchwork quilt.

The afternoon sun beamed through the kitchen window and onto the large table where we prepare the food. It made a fine spot to lay my patchwork and the basket of scraps. Today, while choosing my next piece of cloth, I became lost in memories as I laid three on the table.

The first, a rectangle of blue wool, came from the dress my mother had been wearing in the days before she died. I didn't have the whole dress, that having been reworked into one to fit Little Lucy, but I kept a panel cut from the back when it was taken in. The next came from a dress all three of us sisters wore as small girls. When the garment could be remade no more, it had been placed into mother's basket of memories. More recently, I had taken it and cut out pieces of material the colour of willow leaves, leaving the seams and ties in the basket. The last was a remnant from a dress Ma made Kitty from beige woollen cloth with a fine brown stripe. She kept a length of it, expecting to change the hem before long but, for some reason lost in time, she never did. I looked at all three, placed them beside the last russet-coloured square, and chose the willow green.

I expect ladies spend their time decorating their clothes with fancy trimmings, and I do have bits of lace and ribbon in the basket, but my oddments are the story of my childhood and are mostly plain linen and woollen cloth. They are rich with memories and give me much pleasure. Sometimes I have thoughts of my husband asking what this one and that one means to me, and me telling him about my years growing up along Five Vents Lane here in Old Romney. I can't see him clearly because I'm not courting, and he's not real to me yet.

"Hello Mary. Busy sewing." Reverend Kenelm said, startling me as I concentrated on hemming a neat square. "What's this you're working on?"

"Oh, sir, you surprised me." My heart raced uncomfortably. "I didn't hear you coming. I've done your repairs. This is my patchwork. I'm hemming squares." I indicated three in a row on the table.

"Your patchwork?"

"It's nothing special," I bumbled. "At least not to other people. But it is to me because these are my mother's scraps."

"What are you making with them?" he asked in his kindly manner.

"A cover for my bed so, when I look at it, I can picture Ma and us girls wearing all these different materials. The dresses got too small, or old and tatty, you see. But there are still some bits left that can be useful."

"Will it be all squares?"

"It won't. The centre will be a star with eight points and made from material Ma was given by her Aunt Wilcocks." I blushed a little, hoping he didn't hear the pride in my voice, but persevered with the details. "It's blue, you see. Not from woad, which is what you'd expect, but from indigo."

"Indigo!" The rector sounded impressed. "I'll look forward to seeing your star."

What a thoughtful man. I returned to my sewing, once more thankful for my good fortune in being taken on as a maid at the rectory. I expected him to move on, perhaps to his desk, but he didn't, so I ventured to ask, "When exactly is the archbishop coming?"

"In six days. And it's thanks to you that the roof of our Lady Chapel is being repaired. There are three men working on it now."

"Oh, that's wonderful, sir. I am pleased."

There was something else pleasing me. I had noticed that the rector had been standing a little taller on this last day since we heard about the archbishop coming. Whereas before he walked like an older man, his gait ponderous and head lowered, now his pace had quickened as he bounded along. These past six months, it seemed as if he couldn't summon the enthusiasm for anything, and now I saw a sense of urgency. It was all thanks to the visitation from Archbishop Parker.

What will the archbishop make of our humble church? I wondered again and again. "Will there be a party of women going to clean the church?" I asked. In the past, my mistress had gathered a group together and seen to it that the floors were swept and scrubbed, the wood waxed, and cobwebs brushed away. Now any efforts were half-hearted. The women of Old Romney needed to be led, and their leader had passed to a better place.

"What a good idea, Mary!" he replied. "You're a sensible girl – I'll leave it for you to organise."

I turned pink with pleasure, unable to find the words to answer the rector, and concentrated on putting my scraps of material back in the basket. There would be no more time for sewing now.

"On Sunday, I'll go to Midley," the rector told me, continuing our conversation. "The curate remains in bed."

"Do you know what ails him?"

"His chest is weak. Goodwife Beth takes him thin broth every day. He cannot summon the strength to eat anything heartier."

"There is much goodness in broth," I replied with confidence. Then my thoughts flitted to Midley. "You said Archbishop Parker will go to Midley?"

"He will."

"But what about the man who lives in the church? Him who washes the bodies?"

"What would I do without you, Mary?" The rector's voice rose while his face was a picture of dismay. "I must go there before Sunday and see this man. He must be gone before the archbishop arrives."

"You're going to be busy," I observed. *It will do you good. I am sure of it.*

"I am and, before the treks to Midley, I'd best write a sermon." He turned to leave the kitchen. "I'll be at my desk."

I watched him leave. *Aye, you should write your sermon, and I should be thankful that you have remembered it. There have been times when I thought I would have to write it for you and, whatever Margery says, I do not have the learning to do that.*

Avery

I have a small bench which I move about, depending on the weather and where I want to sit. On Sunday, I place it facing Lydd and, in my thoughts, I join the congregation in their long church with its tall tower. On dry, breezy days I put the bench in a place where the old stone walls of the church can offer a buffer from the wind. On a summer's day, when I am looking for a cool spot, I use those ancient walls to shade me from the sun.

This morning, the bench had been placed in the corner between the tower and the western wall of the church. With a pail of water at my feet, my cloak, jerkin and breeches beside me, I kept busy spot-cleaning the clothes. Women's work, some may think. I have no wife or maid to serve me, so all work is my work.

From here I watched the rector approaching along the trackway from Bell Corner, his pace slow, telling me this was not a man used to long days of physical activity. At first, he didn't notice me, but when he finally did, I raised a hand to acknowledge him. Then I continued with my task, only standing to greet him as he crossed a narrow dyke and walked the last steps towards the church.

"Good day!" he called.

"Good day," I repeated. Although we had not met before, I sensed who he was and did not welcome him to Midley, as it was already his place. In the time I had been here it had always been the curate who came, and he gave me no bother.

"Reverend Edward Kenelm," he stated. "Rector of Old Romney and Midley."

"Avery Bridgeman."

We stood facing each other, me still standing in the shadows of the church and him on the sandy slope which, over the years, has been referred to as the 'nose' of Midley. I moved a little, so I no longer stood on higher ground, but kept the distance between us.

"The archbishop is coming," the rector declared without preamble. "He wants to see this church and all the others on the Marsh. He wants to keep an eye on the place."

"I met Archbishop Parker when he visited three years ago," I told him. "I was at Newchurch then."

"You met him?" He couldn't hide the surprise in his voice. "At Newchurch?"

"Aye."

"You mean to say that you saw him? From a distance?"

"Nay, I showed him the church. I was a lay preacher, then curate there for a time."

I expect it is a rare thing to render a clergyman speechless, but this is what happened.

Without offering him a seat or a cup of wine, I began my story. "I came from Rochester," I told him, and my thoughts shifted to a wide expanse of tidal Medway, a square castle overlooking the river, a cathedral, and streets bursting with life – from beggars to traders and innkeepers, priests and gentry. "My father was a vintner, with warehouses and a pontoon for the ships which delivered wine to him before sailing upriver to London. He paid for me to go to the grammar school in the city, where I was educated by priests. By the time I was fourteen, I had decided that my future lay in the Church. There was not the money to send me to Oxford, so it was arranged for me to be the server to a vicar in Chatham. When I reached seventeen years of age, I was sent further afield to continue my training – to Newchurch, here on Romney Marsh.

"At twenty, I journeyed back to Rochester to see my family for the first time in three years. I carried good tidings – the Archbishop of Canterbury had agreed that I could travel to the city and be interviewed. If he was satisfied, then I would be ordained as a priest, and most likely stay on Romney Marsh to serve as curate in one of the parishes that had no incumbent living there."

"You are ordained?" the rector asked. His brow creased, and I could see he was hanging onto my every word.

"Aye, but it took a while longer. While back in Rochester, I strayed from my path as men have strayed throughout history. I met a young woman, fair of skin, with eyes that danced and sparkled, and a tempting curve to her breasts." I paused, realising I had become lost in the moment; my words and thoughts had strayed to needless details. "We married and I took her back to Newchurch as my bride."

"She isn't here now," the rector said. I could tell he knew the next twist to my tale.

"She isn't here now," I confirmed. "The good rector of Newchurch was perturbed by my bringing a wife back with me, but he allowed me to remain in my position as lay preacher, even providing us with a two-roomed cottage which boasted a roof of new thatch. There was no more talk of my being ordained for some time, but eventually I proved myself worthy. We lived happily for just over a year before she succumbed to the Marsh Ague and, while in a weakened state, she was taken by the Black Death."

"I'm sorry," the rector murmured. I sensed he was there with me as I relived the past years.

"I washed my wife's body before she was taken to her final resting place. This was the last service I could do for her, and it soothed my troubled mind to know I'd taken tender care of her.

"A few days later, I washed an old man who had also suffered from the plague. I, who had been so close to it, remained untouched. Unable to settle in Newchurch, I left one night and found myself at St Marys where I washed the body of a boy before he was taken to the plague pit. I found peace in offering this last act of kindness to someone who had suffered so much."

"You didn't catch it?"

"I didn't. But no one wants to be around a man who has been in contact with the Black Death. They want to call on me for my services but they won't welcome me into their community. So, I found this place, this church where no one comes, and I settled here. Your curate knew and allowed me to shelter here. People from Lydd and these outlaying cottages and farms bring me food."

"You're happy. Happy here at Midley?" he asked.

I turned back to look at the old church walls – a curious mixture of stone and brick. My gaze roamed to the row of small, unglazed windows and then to the slim tower with its dishevelled spire. "I'm happy with my role in this life," I replied. "I've known better places to shelter, but being here gives me peace. There are stories to be discovered about this church. I see hints of it in the stones and bricks, and in the stone face which gazes along the nave, but I don't know the history of the building."

"Do you miss the company of other men and women?" the rector queried.

I considered this carefully before replying: "I think one day I will. But I'm content here."

All this time, I stood in the shadows of the tower and western wall and the rector stood nearby, also shaded by the church. Now he began a circuit of the building, first walking towards the chancel end and pausing to look at the window. I trailed behind him.

"What happened to the glass?" he asked.

"I don't know."

"The shingles have fallen."

I looked up at the open patches of roof, then down at the wooden tiles on the ground. "It's not too bad inside. The roof could be patched."

"When the curate comes to take a service, does anyone come?"

"Rarely. No one lives hereabouts and those that do go to Lydd, Brookland or Old Romney. I sit outside and listen the best I can. It is the closest I'll get to attending."

"I'll go inside now," the rector said, an eye on the fragile spire. "Alone."

I nodded and watched him step through the open archway into the base of the tower which also served as a porch. It was not difficult to imagine the rector's dismay when he saw the earth where floor tiles had once laid, the small windows bare of shutters and the glorious chancel window empty of all glass. The remaining prayer books and bibles were damp, the altar cloth nothing but a rag, and there were no candles left to burn. Had they been there, I would have kept a candle lit and it would have offered me comfort. Amongst all the decay, I knew he would not notice that I kept the floor swept clean and had cleared the dead birds and mammals away.

"Where are the plate, the candlesticks and the alms box?" Reverend Kenelm asked when he joined me in the sunshine.

"I've never seen them," I told him.

"They were in a trunk," he said.

"I would never look in a trunk that was not mine to open."

"I believe you," he said. "You're an honest man."

"For now, I have found my place in this world."

He acknowledged my words with a slow nod and continued, "There is nothing to be done about this place and no funds for me to spend on it. I must concentrate on St Clement's and face the archbishop's wrath when he sees how I have allowed this church to go to ruin."

"May God look kindly upon you," I murmured, understanding his concerns.

"Thank you," he replied. "You'll have to go. You know that, don't you?"

I gazed up at the church – the place which had become a place of sanctuary for me despite its flaws.

"I understand."

We didn't speak about whether I would return to Midley after the visitation. Perhaps he assumed I would, or maybe we both knew my time here was over.

Reverend Edward Kenelm left after that. He said he planned to visit some of the farms in the parish. The last I saw of the rector, he was taking a narrow path towards that raised track they call Midley Wall.

I stood, bathed in bright summer sunlight, watching him for a while, then turned and stepped into the cool, musty church. Inside, I gazed up at the carved stone face. "I'll be going tomorrow and don't know if I'll be back," I said. "I thought I'd be here a bit longer, but instead you'll have Archbishop Parker's company." The face gazed unseeingly past me.

Avery

Today I prepared to leave Midley for the coast and a place I had heard of but never ventured. It saddened me that I would no longer tend the dead hereabouts, but life was taking me in a new direction, and I felt curious to know what was in store.

My few belongings were placed in a neat row along a bench, and my rolled blankets propped against the wall. I placed my spare shift and hose, my comb, spoon, beaker and bowl in a hessian sack. Then I picked up the blankets and, with my hand, swept away the fragments of limewash and flakes of plaster which fell persistently from the church walls.

Before leaving, I nodded towards the stone face. "Goodbye." I am not a foolish man – I did not expect a response – but some days this face staring into the distance was the best company I had. Into the sunlight I went, for it was another glorious day, and with one last glance at the dilapidated church, I set off towards Lydd.

Once near the town, I skirted the cluster of houses until I met a couple of fishermen with a horse and cart. "Is this the road to Dengemarsh?" I asked.

"Aye," they said in harmony.

"Stay on this track and you'll soon have the taste of salt on your lips," one continued. "Then you'll be at Denge."

"Have you got business there?" the second asked.

I shrugged. "Nay, I'm just interested to see new places."

They frowned, not knowing what to make of that, but the cart contained baskets of fish for sale, and they moved on.

I left Lydd behind me and followed the stony track, noting that the grass in the fields grew sparsely, and there were patches of ground with nothing much for the sheep to nibble at. By the time I reached a group of three farms, the fields were clearly lacking in soil, the surface thick with stones. Despite this, rows of cabbages thrived, goats roamed, and, to my surprise, I noted enclosures filled with large, ugly birds. A man, swarthy and with a look of discontent, trundled a barrow along the fence line. He nodded in my direction, and I raised my hand in greeting.

"There's no work here," he said.

"I'm not looking for work," I replied. "Is this the track to Denge?"

"You've reached Denge."

I digested the news and couldn't help feeling curious about the place. This inhospitable land was somehow supporting three farms, two of them boasting substantial brick farmhouses and the third a fair-sized cottage.

"What do you farm here? How do you manage?" I found myself asking before I could stop myself.

"Turkeys and goats, as you can see," he said. "And greens but not root vegetables. We fish from the pits and keep pigs in the holly wood over yonder." I followed his gaze inland and to the west.

"It must be a hard life."

He narrowed his almost black eyes, drawing thick bushy brows together and said, "I keep my eyes peeled for new opportunities."

I knew then that I had met someone who would not settle for what life had offered him but would take his chance with something new. This fellow, whose name I never learnt, was not so unlike myself.

"If I keep walking, I'll reach the coast?" I asked.

"You will," he said, and with that he turned his back on me, muttering to himself as he took a mallet from the barrow and set about repairing the fence.

I continued, having found out no more about Denge and uncertain if I was heading in the right direction. However, I remembered the words of the fishermen I had met upon leaving Lydd, and I could taste the salt on the breeze, although the sea remained elusive. In no time at all, any fencing or field marking had gone, and with them the grass and cabbages. Now a shingle landscape rolled along in dips and rises, with very few plants growing. *No wonder when there is no soil. None at all. This can't be right. I must have been misled. Surely there is nothing to be found at the end of this track.*

Yet there was something. Just as the band of sparkling grey-blue sea came into view, I spotted a couple of squat buildings – could these be the hovel and the chapel which the rector of Newchurch had told me about? I picked up my pace.

In a dip before the shingle rose and dropped toward the beach, I found the spot I was seeking. There had been a time, perhaps thirty years before, when a hermit had lived at Dungeness and cared for a chapel dedicated to St Mary. I had discussed this at length with my friend, the rector of Newchurch, as it had been recorded in the annals of history by King Henry's men. He had never seen the place for himself, but it had been the topic of conversation several times. For some reason, it was the first place I thought of when told to leave Midley, and I found myself determined to seek refuge there.

The hermitage still stood – what a relief, as I had nowhere else to shelter overnight. My first impressions were that it was a sturdy little place made of rubble stone and beach pebbles. The roof was tiled, probably because thatch would have soon yielded to the sea winds. It lacked windows, and the doorway faced the land. I could see the opening as I approached and immediately noticed that the door had either rotted away or been taken for some other purpose. Before peeping into the hovel, as it had been called by the rector of Newchurch, I walked towards the chapel.

At first, I wondered if the holy place had fallen or been taken down, but then I realised it had never been a complete building to start with. The altar remained with a wooden cross at the centre and two unlit candles, all within a solid, semi-circular stone wall standing about six feet high. The hermit could have worshipped and, I assumed, the chapel served its purpose while giving some shelter. Pausing for a moment, I bowed my head, offered a prayer for the soul of the hermit and gave my thanks for his humble home where I planned to stay for a few days.

Next, I went to explore the hermitage. "What's this doing here?" I asked aloud. "Wood – and lots of it." However, there was room for me to lay my blankets and sleep overnight. I could ask for no more. "There must be a reason for it."

Leaving my belongings by the woodpile, I trudged up the shingle bank and took in the full expanse of the bay. A sense of elation filled me – how mighty the sea was and how refreshing the salt air! I realised that I stood almost at the tip of a stony peninsular, with a great bay sweeping around to my right and the same to my left. The beach was at first stones and then sand. In the distance, steep cliffs rose, and I could see no further. Close to the shore, nets and poles were set up to catch fish, and two small vessels were pulled up beyond the high tide mark. Now I understood the reason for the track continuing beyond the farms to the coast and recalled the wagon of fish seen in Lydd. Mesmerised by the movement of the tide, I watched it for some time before noticing a large area of ash on the top of the bank. "Ah! This is why they store wood here. It must be a beacon. Something to warn ships about this bank? Or to bring them to safety. Probably to warn them."

Well, I had arrived and found the place I intended to shelter, but what to do next? My stomach grumbled, and I had some bread and cheese with me, so I returned to the hermitage and retrieved the food. *It's all you have,* I told myself, eyeing the humble meal. *Eat half.* With reluctance, I split the food and wrapped some up for later. Then I returned to the top of the beach and sat, legs outstretched, facing the sea. In time, I began to doze and allowed myself the luxury of an afternoon nap.

When I woke, I was immediately aware of my foolishness in sleeping with the sun's rays beating down upon me. The skin on my nose and cheeks felt tight and hot to touch. I walked to the sea and cupped handfuls of salt water, sloshing it over my face several times. Feeling refreshed, and liking the taste of salt on my lips, I turned back and clambered up the steep, stony bank.

"What next?" I asked myself. I had found my shelter but had very little food and just a clay flask of weak ale. The rector had been fascinated by the tales of this desolate headland and reports of the hermit. I knew from our conversations that, unlikely as it may seem, a freshwater spring would be revealed at low tide. "And low tide it is!" I stated with joy. So, back down the bank I went and walked first in the direction of Rye and then back to the tip of the promontory where I found water bubbling from the stones. "But how to capture it?" I pushed some shingle aside and, once more, cupped my hands, this time using them to drink from. "I'll bring a dish later."

Scrambling up the bank again, I realised that the long-gone hermit had built his home and chapel close to the water source. "He chose wisely," I murmured to myself.

The rest of the afternoon was spent moving wood in the hermitage so, when I settled for the night, I could be sure it would not tumble upon me. Then I took a long, slender stick, sharpened one end to a point, and headed for the drainage ditch running alongside the track to Lydd. It took a while for me to negotiate the steep banks and to perch in a spot right next to the water, but the rewards from this ditch were worth the effort – it teemed with eels. Catching one proved tricky, and I failed again and again. Finally, my spear hit the spot and pressed through the flesh; I lifted the writhing eel and flung it onto the ground. A sharp blow with a stone stunned it. Racing, as best I could on the stones, I reached the ashes on the beach. Then I rolled the eel in suffocating ash, leaving it for a couple of hours.

Late in the day, just before sunset, the low sun lent a richness in colour to the stones. Those which were pale brown became burnished gold, and those which were grey became polished pewter. The sea, now rising to its full height, rolled towards me, a deep blue-grey.

I managed to tempt a small fire to burn in the remains of what I assumed was a beacon, then brushed off the ash, skewered the eel and set about roasting it. As dusk fell, and I began to feel as if I were the only person on this headland, I heard footsteps steadily approaching on the shingle. There was nothing to be done about hiding, and no need to, so I stood to face the men.

"We heard there was someone down here," one said.

"And wondered what your business was," the other continued.

"I'm not after any trouble. Just shelter for a couple of nights," I answered. "I'm Avery."

"Avery from where?" the first asked.

I considered this before answering. "Rochester originally, then Newchurch for several years and now... now I go here and there."

They seemed to accept this, nodding slowly.

"This is where you make a fire," I stated. "A beacon, is it?"

"Aye. Keeps the boats off the point, it does. Dangerous waters out there. They're grateful to us for keeping it burning."

"And if it happens to go out?"

"Let's get the wood. Fire's getting low."

My question was ignored. Perhaps because their attention had turned to the job in hand, perhaps because they chose to dismiss it.

That evening, we sat around the beacon, and they spoke about their lives farming the inhospitable land around the three farms – Dengemarsh Court, Harts and Brickwall. If they held back on telling me some of their secrets (and there were secrets to be told – I was sure of it) then no wonder as I was still a stranger to them. In turn, I refrained from divulging the very thing that would have led them to rejecting my company. For those few hours, as the sky darkened and the stars grew in brightness, I was just a wanderer who happened to be there. They didn't know that only two days before I had tended the body of a plague victim, giving him the respect and care that he had not known in life.

Now I lie in my bed, sometimes hearing the men talking, sometimes hearing the crackle of a fire. A plan has been made between us three: I have agreed to tend the beacon for however long I choose to remain here. In turn, the women of Dengemarsh will bring me meals twice a day. It is a plan which suits us all nicely. I will be fed and know that I am welcome here. They can tend their crops and animals without having the burden of a night spent by the beacon.

I am hoping that while being in this place, with the sound of the sea pounding in my head and the tang of salt air on my lips, I'll reflect on my choices since my young wife died and consider cutting a new path.

Kitty

The mistress has been making such a fuss. She's had enough of our floor here at Wheelsgate being half tiled and half bare earth. I've had enough of it too – but it's not my place to complain. Every day once, twice, three times… I must sweep and scrub earth from the tiles.

"We'll put rushes down," the master has said at least once a day for the past six months.

"I'm not putting rushes down when we are halfway to having a tiled floor," she replies every time.

In the last few weeks, the mistress has come up with a new plan: "You'll have to go to Rye, to the yards there, and get some to match."

He laughed at this. "Me? Me go to Rye when there's sheep to tend and crops to harvest and dykes to clear. Oh no! If he stays into the autumn, when the reeds are cut, then I'll be laying some of them down like we used to."

"Six months he's been here," she mutters to herself every now and then. "It's no place for a young man, is it? He'll be wanting to move on soon."

The mistress is talking about the body washer, of course. Him who comes along and washes the bodies of those who die from the plague. Before he lived in the old church across the fields in Midley, the master and farmhands were helping themselves to the floor tiles in the church. They were not theirs to take. It is not even our church – Wheelsgate is in Old Romney parish – but they took them anyway. The curate walks along to hold a service once a week, even though no one goes to it. I wonder if he noticed that the tiles were slowly vanishing. When someone started living in the church, the mistress said they should carry on taking the tiles. They didn't belong to that young man, she decided. Then they learnt that he'd been touched by the Black Death. Not only had his own wife died from it but he went courting it when he decided to wash the bodies of the dead. So, that put a stop to taking any more tiles from Midley church.

Today the mistress had news to share about the body washer. "He's gone!" she announced, as she trimmed the turnips.

"Who's gone?" I asked, busy slicing leeks.

"That young man who was living in the church."

"Oh! Where's he gone?"

"I don't know and what does that matter? One of the lads said he was seen leaving yesterday. We can start lifting the tiles again and this floor will be done by Michaelmas."

"That will be a fine thing," I said, knowing it would please her.

We continued with our washing and chopping, then tipping vegetables into the big pan. The mistress cut some herbs, and I added more fresh water. Then she gave it a stir and asked, "Have you seen your sister? The quiet one?"

"Lucy? Nay, you said she wasn't to come here until the plague passed, and that was about ten weeks ago. My other sister, Mary, saw her once at Old Romney, but that was a month or more ago."

"He must have washed her body then," the mistress stated as if she was talking about a lamb or a pig gone to slaughter, not my younger sister.

"I suppose he did."

I felt a bit sad then. Lucy was a simple soul but never meant any harm. I'd been harsh with her the last time we'd met in the lane. Silly of her to come visiting when she'd been living alongside the plague, but I'd let my sharp tongue run away with me. I was always like that with her, while she was nothing but sweet and kind to me.

"She might not have got it... got the plague," I suggested.

"But she's not been to visit on a Sunday, has she?"

"She hasn't," I admitted, feeling foolish. Lucy would not have changed her habits. On Sunday she went to church and walked along to Wheelsgate. She did what was expected of her. "I'll speak to my other sister about it," I said, not wanting to talk about Lucy with the mistress. "I'll be glad to be sweeping and scrubbing tiles. It will look fine once the men have laid them."

The mistress nodded. I tried very hard to think about the tiles and not Lucy in the plague pit.

Mary

This morning, I felt proud to be sitting in the church with Reverend Kenelm's cook, Goodwife Beth, beside me and Goodwife Margery on the bench behind. Margery's husband wasn't there but, if I twisted in my seat and peered around the pillar, I could see the Lady Chapel roof had been repaired. The reason for my pride was that the rector stood taller, and his words came across more forcefully than in the last six months. He wore his surplice – the one with the newly turned and stitched hem. As he preached and prayed, and we offered our responses, I felt that our rector looked younger and more confident than he had since his dear wife died. *It is partly due to my care and encouragement,* I said to myself during the service. *Archbishop Parker will think good of him. At least I hope he will.*

Afterwards, the rector stood at the doorway to the porch and spoke to every person as they filed out. Instead of going straight back to the rectory, I walked a slow circuit around the church, lingering at times. The first place I paused was the only spot in the churchyard where I could look across the fields to the church at Hope. *It's in a poor state, they say, with only three houses in the whole parish. I wonder what Archbishop Parker will think of that.* An uncharitable thought came to mind: *If he goes there first, then he won't think so badly about us here in Old Romney with our fifteen homes.*

I continued, pausing to gaze at the old yew – its trunk so wide that, as children, it would take two of us to reach around it, our fingers just touching. Smiling at the memory, I stopped at my parents' plain wooden cross and had a quick word with them. "Hello Ma. Hello Pa. I'm nicely settled here with the rector. He treats me well and I keep my eye on him, making sure he's turned out nicely for church. Kitty is happy, although she wasn't in church this morning. I expect she was needed back at Wheelsgate. She'll be along later. I don't know about Lucy. We haven't heard from her, and she usually calls on Kitty. It's been a while. Four or five weeks, I think, since I saw her."

I felt a lump rise in my throat and tears threatened. Turning, I walked back to the church porch, trying to breathe slowly and deeply. The rector stood outside now, and I think he noticed I was not quite myself.

"Ah, there you are, Mary."

"I've been to see my parents, sir. I go to have a word with them every now and then."

He nodded, and I knew he understood because he often visited his wife. "I'm going to Midley now," he reminded me.

"I hope someone goes to worship there," I replied, even though I knew no one would.

"The day after tomorrow the archbishop comes," he said. "At least I can tell him that I've done my best by the people of Midley."

"They are not godless folk," I reminded him. "They just choose to go to some other place. Lydd, I think."

"I'm sure you're right." With this he crossed the churchyard and took a footpath across a field. I stayed by the church porch and watched as he reached a cluster of cottages and disappeared from sight.

I stared into the distance for a while, there being no one to distract me. Then I thought about the rector arriving at the old church, finding it empty, and returning disheartened. Without giving it any more thought, I followed in his footsteps.

It was a while before I spotted him again and I think I had gained on him. By now the cottages and farms of Old Romney were behind me and the land lay open before me. Reverend Kenelm left the track we call Swamp Lane and took the path to the old church. Still some way behind, I trotted along, keeping an eye on him. He never looked back, and by the time I left Swamp Lane, he was trudging up the rise to the church. In time, I reached the slope, and he had passed out of sight.

The sun shone in a near cloudless sky, and I had been walking without thought of a drink or stopping to rest in the shade. With my sleeve, I wiped the sweat from my brow and suddenly felt exhausted. How foolish to set off without taking a flask of weak ale. I gazed to the north-west – the farmhouse, cottages and barns at Wheelsgate shimmered in the sunshine. *I could go and call on Kitty – but it's some distance.* I gazed to the south and a small place called Swamp Farm. *I could ask for a drink at the farm.* Then I looked towards a cluster of trees. *There used to be a farm there, or so I believe. I wonder if there's a well.* I shrugged. *If I go off looking for a drink, then he won't know I came to hear his sermon.* Looking up at the slim tower with its ragged remains of a spire, I took a deep breath and summoned up the energy to walk the last few steps to the church.

It felt cool in the porch, although shafts of warm light filtered past the toppled struts, rafters and wooden shingles which once made a spire. They shone upon sturdy beams, strong enough to hold a bell, and on a jumble of cobwebs, before reaching the floor. The air smelt rich with scents of the farmyard and, looking down, I noted piles of sheep droppings, swept to the sides so the pathway to the church remained clear. Gazing up I wondered what had happened to the church bell and then thought that perhaps there had never been one.

As I placed my hand on the oak door, it moved. Startled, I found myself face to face with Reverend Kenelm. I had expected to find him at the altar.

"Mary!" he exclaimed, a look of pleasure on his face swiftly replaced with concern. "What brings you here?"

"It felt wrong." My heart hammered – partly from the surprise and then from seeing the initial smile on his face. The rector was no longer a man of mature years, as he had seemed during these past six months of mourning, but youthful and with a renewed interest in life. A handsome man and kindly too. "It felt wrong," I started again, "to think of you being here and no one else caring whether or not a Sunday sermon and prayers were said."

"You followed me here!"

"My mother told me her family came from Midley," I answered. "She said we were both Old Romney and Midley."

"Then it's only right that you come and see the old place." He stepped aside, allowing me to walk past him and into the church. The contrasts of light and dark were strong. Light through the empty chancel window and the holes in the roof. Darkness in the corners where broken benches had been piled, and the remnants of the carved rood screen were propped against walls from which lumps of plaster had fallen. I noticed that the floor was almost bare of tiles, yet it had been tiled because some remained and the earth showed a faint pattern of squares. Even the altar had been stripped of any ornament other than a wooden cross and a ragged cloth, which must have once been made with love to lie in pride of place.

"There is no denying I've neglected this church," the rector murmured, now standing beside me.

"Your curate is elderly and no godly person from the parish has come to care for the church," I reminded him. "Instead, they have abandoned it and worse... they have stolen from it."

"Stolen?" he repeated. Then he gazed up to the window and back to the altar. "I suppose you are right. Sometimes a man needs a woman to tell him what is plain to see."

"I don't think it was the man who has been living here," I ventured to say. "I believe he only wanted to do good."

"You are right. He is a good man. He told me his story."

We stood in silence for a moment, it not being my business to question him about the body washer. Eventually, I asked, "What will you do? No one came to the church service."

"I prayed before you arrived and begged the good Lord for guidance," he told me. "Then you came. Now we must head back to Old Romney."

Once outside, with no shade from the sun, I remembered being thirsty during my walk. "Do you know where the farm was? Longhouse, my mother called it. I believe there was a well and…"

"I have wine." He produced a clay flask. "Share some with me? The farmhouse was over there, but I doubt we would find a bucket for the well."

I had never shared a drink with the rector before. But I had never been to Midley church with him and stood talking as if we were friends, not rector and maid. After that we walked back across the field, then along Swamp Lane. He told me a little about the man who washed bodies, and we wondered if he would return to Midley, or find another place to call home. I found myself seeing my rector anew. First, he was rector and husband, then rector and mournful widower. Today he became a man in my eyes, and for the first time I knew how a young woman's heart could flutter when given attention. I wondered if he would truly notice that I could read, write, and sew neatly. Might he be interested to know I could play a tune on a lute?

As we approached the rectory, I slipped back into my role as maid. "I'm going to clean the church tomorrow morning," I told him. "Me and a few of the other women."

"Thank you. Then we will have done all we can to please Archbishop Parker." He took the path leading to the front door.

I turned to walk around to the back of the house, saying as we parted, "Dinner will be mutton chops. It will be ready at the usual time."

"What would I do without you?" he asked.

I paused for a moment, lost for words, but it seemed that he didn't expect an answer as he opened the front door and stepped inside.

Mary

"He's coming today!" Goodwife Beth said as she walked through the open back door. "I've put a clean apron on, and you should too."

"He won't be interested in meeting us," I retorted. "Anyway, my apron is clean. I changed it after sweeping out the hearth." I scowled. I didn't need Beth to tell me what to do. She wasn't in charge of me or the rectory.

"I wonder what time he'll be here." She took a couple of onions and began deftly peeling away the skin. "I'm going to make a pie, but I can't say if the rector will be eating at his usual time. Haven't you started on the bread yet?"

"The rector asked me to iron his surplice," I told her. "The bread had to wait." I smiled to myself – no amount of nagging could spoil my joy in seeing the rector take some pride in his appearance. Beth might cook, but I handled all Reverend Kenelm's sewing and darning with pride.

We worked in silence for a moment: me spooning flour into a bowl, Beth chopping the onions and pushing them off the wooden board and into a pan.

However, the imminent arrival of the archbishop remained in our thoughts, and we soon started chatting again.

"Do you know his plans? The archbishop's, I mean," Beth asked. "Has the rector said? Not that he needs to say to us, but he might have mentioned it… if a letter happened to come."

"A letter was delivered by messenger yesterday afternoon," I replied. "Archbishop Parker and his men are staying in New Romney. This morning he'll come here, then go to Midley. Afterwards he'll go to Lydd."

"He'll be eating a dinner in Lydd then," she decided, "and coming by horse, I suppose."

"It's not my business to know where he'll be eating, but that's what I think. It's what the rector thinks as well."

By then Beth had moved on to chopping turnips. She paused, knife mid-air. "Lordy, young Mary, what's all this about you knowing what the rector thinks?"

I kept my attention on the bread dough. "I'm just saying. It makes sense, doesn't it?"

By the time Beth was adding carrots to the pan, she had more to say: "I think he's an elderly gent. I heard it somewhere. Worked for the old king, he did."

"And then for Queen Mary?" I asked.

"Of course not," Beth scoffed. "All your darning and fussing around the rector… Has none of his learning rubbed off on you?"

My cheeks burned. Usually I enjoyed her company, but today it seemed that Beth was intent on riling me.

"She was Catholic. You should know – you being named after her."

"I wasn't thinking."

We went our own ways after that. Goodwife Beth stayed in the kitchen making a pastry top for the pie and starting on a pan of broth, before preparing strawberries to be used for jam making. I gathered my brush and pan, cleaning rags and polish, then went upstairs to see to the rector's bedroom and the little square of a landing. Smiling to myself, I knew I had the best vantage place in the village and, if I took my time brushing down the curtains and bed hangings, there was a chance of me seeing Archbishop Parker arrive.

I happened to be standing on a stool, dusting all the crevices where the ceiling met the walls and spiders liked to lurk, when I spotted a party of gentlemen riding along Five Vents Lane towards our village. Without pausing to watch their progress or to see what I could learn about them from afar, I jumped off the stool, dropped my duster on the floor and hurried downstairs. I had to ensure the rector made a good impression on this important day.

"They're coming. Almost here!" My words rushed at Beth as I tore through the kitchen.

"Your shawl!" she almost screamed at me. "Make yourself decent, girl."

My cheeks burned to think of the archbishop seeing me in just my light dress which was no more than a shift. These summer days were warm, and upstairs in the rectory the air felt thick with both the rising heat from the kitchen fire and the warmth from the relentless sunshine. At the open back door, I swivelled around, grabbed my shawl from the back of a chair, and then dashed to the well. The lad who did outside jobs had left a bucket of cool, fresh water on the ground. I dipped my cupped hands in it and sloshed it over my face. My whole body shivered.

"Enough racing about, Mary," I said to myself as I set off to St Clement's.

Before entering the church, I noticed the rector kneeling at his wife's grave. I faltered, not wanting to disturb him but needing to pass on the news. Fortunately, he saw me and stood, bowed his head towards her headstone and walked towards me.

"I've seen them from the upstairs window," I told him. "Coming by horse." Before the rector could reply, the sound of horses' hooves could be heard on the track leading past the rectory to the church.

"Thank you, Mary," he replied, his tone gentle. "I must go to greet them." With this he swept past me, the folds of his surplice brushing against my own thin skirt, his back straight and stride youthful.

How you have changed in these last few days, I thought. *Is it partly due to the care I show you? Are you learning to live without your wife and look to the future?*

My questions remained unanswered, and now the party from Canterbury were in full view. Five men on horseback spilled across the path, and the first, a gentleman wearing a white shirt with extravagant layers of material at the collar and a rich blue cloak over his shoulders, dismounted with ease, handing the reins to a village lad. He bowed in the direction of Reverend Kenelm and turned to take the reins of the next horse, a beautiful white mare with dappled shoulders and rump. Two other gentlemen, both as well-dressed, wearing richly embroidered, sleeveless jerkins, joined the first and they too bowed briefly towards the rector. These must have been attendants, as all their attention now focussed on an elderly gentleman astride the white mare.

This must be him. This must be the Archbishop of Canterbury!

The last man now came rushing forward with a sturdy stool, and those wearing jerkins supported the archbishop while he dismounted. Then he stood, raised by the stool, held steady by his attendants and surveying our good rector, while Reverend Kenelm bowed deeply before him.

I had imagined Archbishop Parker to be a grand character, bedecked in rich cloth, perhaps carrying a crozier. So, I must admit to being surprised. His dress was plainer than that of his men and, in many ways, he looked to be a lesser man than them. However, what he lacked in sumptuous clothing and youthful vigour, he gained in his aura of importance. The archbishop made a stout figure, standing there as he cast his first judgements upon our village. His eyes were pale, his nose bulbous and red – Goodwife Beth would have muttered about his diet being too rich and fine wine flowing too freely in his chambers at Canterbury. Jowls wobbled and a hand, resting on the shoulder of an attendant, trembled. On thinning white hair, he wore a bonnet – a soft hat of black velvet. A white linen shirt swathed his body, and this was topped with a long, black waistcoat.

Still elevated, the archbishop allowed his gaze to fall on me standing in the churchyard and staring straight at him. My cheeks burned with the shame of being caught idling my time away. I dipped into a brief curtsey and fled to the edge of the churchyard, then slipped through a gap in the hedge and into the kitchen garden of the rectory.

Racing to the back door, I only slowed as I entered the house and said to Beth, "The bread will have risen by now." Then I took the bowl of dough from its warm place by the hearth and prepared it for the bread oven.

"You've seen them," Goodwife Beth stated. "The archbishop and his men."

"I had to tell the rector." I tried to justify my rushing about the place.

"The rector doesn't need some bit of a girl telling him what to do. I saw you, Mary. I saw you from the front window."

"I only went to tell him, and he does need someone keeping an eye on him. You know how it's been since he lost his wife."

"Then you stood staring, and he saw you... the archbishop himself saw you." Beth busied herself stirring the broth, then added another log to the fire, carefully pushing it into place.

"I didn't mean to stare."

"Well, never mind about that. All this fuss over the visit has perked our rector up no end, and that can only be for the good. He'll be looking for a new wife soon, then we'll have a mistress, and everything will be just as it should be. It's all very well, you and me running the place, but he needs a guiding hand."

I didn't reply to that. There was no need. Beth didn't understand how I helped the rector, sometimes listening to him read parts of his sermon or encouraging him to prepare for church. She only came to do the cooking and had no idea about all the things I did to make his life more comfortable. To her I was just the maid, but to him I was becoming a friend... Someone to confide in... Someone to help him take pleasure in life again.

By the time the rector returned, Beth had gone. I wondered if he would like to tell me about the visit and lingered after serving his dinner, but the meal seemed more important than conversation.

"Was the archbishop disappointed in Midley?"

"I found him to be understanding." He sank his fork into the pie and rich gravy bubbled to the surface.

"Was anyone else there? From the parish?"

"Just an old looker who happened to be passing by."

"He'll meet others as he travels on to Lydd," I said, my voice rising as I attempted to sound hopeful.

"Maybe. Tell Beth this pie is delicious."

"Beth has gone, sir. I'll tell her tomorrow." With this I slipped from the room.

We will enter a period of waiting now, returning to our usual routines but without the anticipation of the visitation. I wonder how my rector will be – if he will return to his usual glum ways, or if a new zest for life has taken hold. He is a young man, both in good health and handsome too, and I can only pray that he is ready to lead his flock at Old Romney once more. But I am getting carried away with my words when what I truly wish for is that our friendship, which began at Midley and strengthened as we walked the paths back home, can continue to grow here in a place where he has known such sadness.

Mary

It has been a day much the same as any other. The excitement of Archbishop Parker and his men being here has ebbed as they left for other places, to meet other people and see other churches. One day soon a messenger will come, and we will hear what he thought of our village, but not yet.

My morning chores were the usual – putting the kettle on to boil and taking a jug of warm water up to the rector, then sweeping the hearth and preparing his porridge for breakfast. After that, I emptied his chamber pot and polished some of the heavy oak furniture. Later, I spent time outside, weeding the vegetable plots and foraging in the hedgerows for blackberries.

In the middle of the day, I served Reverend Kenelm his dinner in the front parlour as always. He seemed cheerful enough. However, by suppertime, when I placed a bowl of broth, bread and cheese before him, he barely acknowledged me.

I ate my own meal in the kitchen, returning to find the rector's food untouched.

"Is it not to your liking?" I asked.

"Not to my liking?" He seemed dazed.

"The broth," I replied. "Or are you chilly? It is still August, I know, but I am finding the evenings are cooler. Should I start laying the fire in here?"

"Everything is fine," he answered. "At least as fine as it can be when I have no companion to share my thoughts with."

I could only guess that after the excitement of the archbishop coming my rector had nothing else to make him look to the future, and it was all too easy to return to his morose habits. Unable to comment on his grieving for his wife, I asked, "Would you like me to reheat the broth?"

He looked at it and picked up his spoon. "Mary, it makes no difference to me. I'll eat it as it is, if it pleases you."

I left him for a while. When I returned, the bowl was empty, the bread and cheese half eaten. Usually, he would have retreated to an armchair, but the rector remained at the table.

"Shall I take this away?" I asked.

"Are you pleased, Mary? Are you pleased that I ate some more?"

I noticed the brandy bottle was now on the table. Knowing how the rector liked a glass or two of brandy, I hoped it had improved his mood. "I'm pleased," I said.

"I do need company, but I have been amiss." He stood suddenly, his chair shaking madly before settling back into place. "I have company here with my good Mary who has been so caring and helpful."

"Thank you, sir." I reached for the plate and bowl. As I leaned forward, he swooped, placing a hand on my arm, surprising me so that I jerked upright, letting the dishes fall back onto the table. Then, without any sweet words, he placed his lips on mine, kissing me firmly until my lips parted, and I responded with rising pleasure. After a moment, he stopped and moved back slightly. I expected him to apologise and to beg forgiveness, but our eyes met, and he said nothing. Then he kissed me again, more gently this time while both hands cupped my bottom. The lingering embrace seemed to go on forever and I found myself transported to the meadows around the old church at Midley, to that other time when we were no longer master and maid. I imagined us meeting there secretly and indulging in hours of sharing our dreams and life stories, while holding hands and punctuating the talk with kisses.

My dear rector paused, moving back slightly, one hand now resting on my waist. "What pretty golden hair you have," he murmured, running a finger through my tumbling curls which had escaped their ribbon. "No wonder that you do not have it covered. It should be on show for all to see... for me to see and admire."

"It is uncovered," I whispered, "because I am not wed."

"Not *yet* wed," he replied.

My heart swelled – I did not know such a thing was possible. We had moved beyond the realms of my romantic imaginings and beyond Kitty's foolish chattering about shared kisses with farmhands and the blacksmith's lad. This moment with my rector was more powerful. His lips pressed upon mine again, and I stumbled backwards, him following until he had me pressed against the doorframe, then his lips were on my neck, his teeth nipping. One hand had become tangled in my hair while the other, by accident, slipped under my skirt and was clasped upon my thigh. The doorframe dug into my back, his kisses met mine once more and his tongue flicked into my mouth, and all thoughts of sun-drenched meadows vanished.

My rector paused, but I saw in his eyes that his passion was in no way abated. I shifted a little, easing the discomfort from the doorframe, and his hands settled on my waist again.

"I must go to offer my evening prayers," he murmured. Then he kissed me once more, gently this time.

I wondered if he meant me to go with him to the church, but instead I gathered the supper plate, bowl and cutlery, placing it on a tray.

"I'll eat that now!" my rector announced with glee, snatching at the last of the bread and cheese. "My appetite is quite restored."

I tidied the kitchen then settled at the table, the warm glow of the evening sun casting its rays upon my patchwork. The light was not strong enough for delicate work, but I could still sew a straight line. My thoughts strayed to a time in the future when my bedcover would be complete – telling the story of three sisters and their dear mother.

While I stitched, the rector returned, and I pictured him sitting in his armchair nursing a brandy. When I could sew no longer, I remained at the table, lost in thought with the patchwork before me. It was only when I heard the scrape of his chair and then footsteps, that I stood and began to pack my material, threads and needles away.

"Ah, your patchwork," he said from the kitchen door, standing tall and with a smile on his handsome face.

"It is too dark to continue," I replied needlessly.

"Well, goodnight."

I thought he was going to turn back into the hallway, and he did take a step back, but then my rector faltered. Stepping forward, he dropped a light kiss on the top of my head. I turned my face towards him, hungry for more. For a moment we kissed with all the passion I had experienced earlier before he broke away.

"Goodnight, sweet Mary."

I watched him leave, then busied myself with my last chores before bedtime.

I am sitting on the bed in my room which is no more than a cupboard. Sleep will not come easy tonight – if at all. My lips burn, my face feels raw, but my heart is full. I won't be sleeping in this windowless place for much longer. But how long is 'for much longer'? Perhaps a month, perhaps two. My rector has shown that he appreciates my care of him over the last six months. I will be the first of us three sisters to marry, and how well I shall marry!

Mary

This morning, as Beth and I busied ourselves with chores, I glimpsed my rector occasionally. When he left for the church, I happened to be in the garden and like to think, in fact I am sure, he had a spring to his step.

After dinner, while I was turning our freshly washed linens and feeling pleased with how well they were drying in the summer sun, a girl came to the back door.

"Can I help?" I called, as I shook the creases from my shift.

She darted over to me. "It's the curate. His wife is asking for Reverend Kenelm – he's taken a turn for the worse."

"And she wants to see the rector?" I checked.

"Aye, she does." She glanced towards the house.

"I'll go and tell him," I answered. An image of the nearby plague pit flashed into my mind. "It's not... He's not got the... The Black...?" I could not bear to utter the word, the very thought of it was so awful.

"It's not that," she replied, and I believed her because the curate had been ill for some time. The plague did not linger but took its victims quickly.

"I'll tell him now," I said, leaving the linens and heading for the house.

My rector was dozing in his armchair, a beaker of wine on a small table beside him. I couldn't help being perturbed to see him like this and had no choice but to wake him. "Sir?" I whispered. He gave no response, so I rapped on the door to the parlour.

"Hello Mary – how can I help you?" He sat up immediately.

Thank the Lord he was just dozing. Memories of the rector spending afternoons in the armchair with nothing but wine for company were still fresh in my mind. Wine and brandy had been his constant companion since he had been left a widower. I hoped those times had passed and he was merely tired. *Perhaps, like me, he had suffered a restless night.* Remembering the reason, I felt a blush rise.

"Mary?"

"Oh, sorry... sorry, sir. It's the curate – there's been a message. He's worse and his wife is asking that you go..."

"Of course," he said, rising from the chair, and nudging the side table. The beaker wobbled and his hand darted to stop it from toppling over. Then he picked up his bible and straightened himself.

He is not drunk. I had lost count of how many times I had cleaned spills from his shirt and breeches or mopped the floor clean.

"I'll go now," he continued, and I moved aside to let him pass. I would have liked it if my rector had paused to gaze at me with affection. Maybe he could have uttered some words complimenting me on my hair or rosy cheeks. However, his thoughts must have been consumed by the ailing curate, as I would expect them to be. For that moment, I was merely the maid.

When he reappeared sometime later, I was standing at the kitchen table folding linen.

"He has little time left in this world," my rector told me from the doorway.

I stepped forward, placing a hand on his arm. "I'm sure your visit gave some comfort."

Seemingly unaware of my closeness, he replied, "I hope so. Is there any supper?" Then he paused, looked me straight in the eyes, smiled a small smile and continued, "How foolish. Of course there is supper."

"Broth with bread and cheese," I told him. "I'll prepare your tray."

We parted, him to the parlour where he would eat alone at the small table, and me to the fireside where the pan of broth simmered. The linen would have to wait.

As dusk falls upon Old Romney, I find myself feeling restless. Memories of yesterday evening and our shared passion fill my mind. But today my rector has not returned since he left to offer his evening prayers in the church. He must have gone back to see the curate, but I do not know. He did not tell me. I am left here, unable to go to bed until he returns, as I must be on hand to offer comfort if he needs it. It is too dark to iron the linens or to sew a neat line of patchwork.

I sit by the fire. I wander outside to watch the sunset. I go to the upstairs window and look across to the church shrouded in darkness, then peep into his bedroom and smooth his bedcover. It is a time of waiting.

Rev. Edward Kenelm

Today is Sunday. Yesterday I buried my elderly curate. Or to be correct, I presided over the grave while others lowered his body, wrapped in cloth, and piled the dry, crumbling earth on top. I merely scattered a handful.

Today is Sunday. Five days since Archbishop Parker graced us with his presence. I am glad he came – thankful he came. I had become a shadow of my former self: morose and disinterested in life. Worse than that, I abandoned my parishioners, so they had no one to guide them, leaving them in the hands of a curate whose life was fast fading away. Now I feel alert, as if woken from a long sleep. My wife and child are gone, and they lie not far from my curate, but I have a sense of purpose once more.

I have a housemaid, named Mary. Not a foolish young girl, but a woman who has tended to my whims, listened to my woes and prompted me to do my duty to God and my people. Without her, my sermons would have suffered, and I might never have left the fireside and my brandy. It is thanks to Mary that, when the archbishop came, he found me in a clean surplice with neat hems.

Now, as I await Archbishop Parker's report on Old Romney and Midley, I am ready to live again.

This morning, when I stood in the churchyard, gazing to the west, Mary joined me. She stayed silently at my side, as if waiting for permission to speak.

"Mary, is there something…?" I asked.

"Just that I wondered if you were going to Midley again?"

"You knew what I was thinking!"

"We went there last week," she reminded me.

"We did, and no one came," I answered. "There's little point, but what if someone did go and found no parson to take the service?"

"I am sure they'd understand," she suggested.

"I think I'll stay here in Old Romney," I decided. "I will pay a call on John Shearer and see what can be done to help while he is unable to work, then come back to the rectory for dinner. There is enough to do here without going about the countryside for no good reason."

John Shearer, a farmer, and I spoke at his kitchen table for a good hour, while his wife plied me with ale and fruit buns. Our talk moved from his family and the farm to our departed curate and the sorry state of the church at Midley.

"You have a curate in the churchyard who is no good to you, and a young man who you have banished from Midley," John observed.

"Not so much banished…"

"He is gone from Midley," the farmer stated. "Here you are, needing a man to help with the care of this parish and Midley, and somewhere nearby there is a curate who was ordained not so long ago."

"That's true."

"Someone who has proven himself to be strong and healthy."

"He certainly seems to be resistant to the plague. You are thinking I could ask him to be my curate?" I asked. "What will the people say?"

"I am not suggesting that he is both body washer and curate. He needs time away from the plague and then people will accept him here. They will be glad to have him!"

"I will be glad to have him!" I grinned at John Shearer.

Since the archbishop's visitation, I have felt old age slipping away from me. Over the past six months I had aged, yet I am no more than twenty-seven years. The parish of Old Romney is small, but Midley stretches out like a finger, all the way to the Sussex border. Now I saw myself riding to the outlying farms to check on the welfare of my people, preparing sermons to engage those huddling in my ancient church and sharing inspiring conversations with my curate.

"It is a fine idea," I declared.

"But he is banished," John said. "Do you know where he went?"

I frowned, trying to recall my time with Avery. "We spoke about Newchurch, but he would not return there. He'd be shunned in any local town or village."

"Is there anywhere he mentioned?"

"A chapel on the headland at Denge."

"Then that's where he will be!"

I considered this for a moment. "He may be. How am I to know?"

"You have a fine mare in your stable. Is there any reason why you can't ride over there now? See if you can find this man?"

My stomach was full of Goodwife Shearer's cake and my appetite for life fully awakened. "I *can* go there now," I declared. "There is nothing to stop me other than my mare being lame."

"Take my horse. He badly needs the exercise."

It had been decided, and I left immediately with promises to let him know the result when I returned with his chestnut gelding.

What a fine day for a ride. I set off in the direction of Swamp Lane, the gelding trotting where the track allowed, while I gazed over hedgerows and across fields, enjoying the view from horseback. Every so often, I passed someone on the lane and occasionally paused to exchange a few words. Lazy cumulus clouds moved slowly across the otherwise blue sky, giving shade from the sun but no threat of rain.

I saw the distant church at Midley, and my thoughts turned to sweet Mary and her following me there just the week before. *She has been a caring presence through these dark months and without her I would have been a sorry sight in front of the archbishop. If she were with me now, I wonder what we would talk about. I wonder what opinions she would share with me.* Just as my imaginings turned to more delightful images of my sweet maid – the adoration in her eyes, the pulse throbbing in her flushed neck and the parting of her curving lips – I heard a woman call, "Reverend Kenelm?"

"Oh... my apologies. I was admiring the... the view," I gabbled.

Stopping for a moment, we spoke of her family and a grandson due to be married. Then, accepting an invitation to stop for a beaker of ale on my return, I urged the gelding into a trot and on we went.

I passed through Lydd, feeling regretful that the shops were closed. Having barely left my small village for so long, I suddenly felt eager to be a part of town life with all the noise and bustle while people went about their business. "There is nothing to stop me from going to New Romney – nothing at all," I murmured to myself while negotiating the narrow roads of Lydd. "The town is no distance, and I cannot believe I have managed so long without it."

From the High Street and Wheeler's Green to an open common known as the Rype, where I urged the chestnut to canter, I rode with a smile on my face and an eagerness to look about the place. It was only as I set off along the stony track towards the coast, that I began to doubt this ride to Denge. Avery had mentioned hearing of a chapel and a shelter by the shingle beach, but there was no knowing if he had headed there or had a change of heart and gone elsewhere. "I should have waited until tomorrow and set off at daybreak, not begun this trek at midday," I told myself. "What was I thinking of when I am expected back for Evensong?"

The only thing I could do, other than turn back, was to ask at the next farm I reached. I felt certain that a stranger would not go unnoticed. It soon became clear the buildings ahead were not one farm, but three houses and all the sheds, barns and shelters needed by farmers. I approached a tall, slim fellow with long white hair, bent over a barrow of cabbages which he pushed along at a steady pace.

"Good afternoon," I called. "Do you live hereabouts?"

"I do," he replied with a merry smile as he straightened himself. "Good afternoon to you, sir."

"Then can you tell me if a stranger has been here recently – a young man with blond hair and striking blue eyes?"

"He's no stranger," the man responded. "The people of Denge welcome any man who will labour beside them in this godforsaken place and especially if he is willing to tend the beacon."

"The beacon?" I repeated.

"On the coast…"

"Of course."

"I was a stranger here once," the man told me. "Perhaps I wouldn't have been shipwrecked if the beacon had been lit that night, but it's a treacherous coastline, so maybe…"

"Where can I find him?" I interrupted.

"He'll be at the hermitage or somewhere nearby."

The hermitage – so the place does exist. I'd long decided it was the stuff of stories. Over the years it had been mentioned, now and then, that in the time of King Henry VIII a hermit had lived on the shingle headland and tended a chapel dedicated to St Mary. *It seems as if our body washer likes dwelling in holy buildings.* I gave a wry smile and turned my attention back to this friendly fellow.

"If I stay on this track, then I'll reach it?"

"You will, and in no time at all. Sir, it's not for me to say but I imagine you have ridden some way. Let me take your horse and he can rest here at Harts Farm while you continue by foot." He gestured towards the nearest and the smallest of the farmhouses.

He could have been nothing but a thief – the chestnut gelding was a fine horse. However, I sensed this man meant well, so I dismounted and handed over the reins. He seemed happy to leave the cabbages where they were for the time being.

"Thank you. I'll come to Harts on my return."

"I'll be looking out for you, but no one is a stranger here for long."

This is a place where everyone is watching and, if I were a betting man, I'd wager that, although it looks empty, a dozen people have seen me from their windows, farmyards or from all manner of hiding places. This land seems flat, but it is ridge after ridge of stones with pits and... I shook myself and asked, "Your name?"

"Pedro, sir."

Odd name – but he said he was from foreign parts. "Reverend Edward Kenelm from Old Romney."

He nodded knowingly. "I thought you were a man of God. You have that look about you."

With that, we went our separate ways, and I continued along the path to the coast, noticing the roar of the sea. After the farms, the landscape was nothing but shingle, with little plant life. Only thick-leaved sea kale grew with vigour. To my left, a drainage ditch took a straight path to the coast, while ahead a ribbon of sea teased me, vanishing with every dip of the path. A small, square building came into view. *Ah! The hermitage.* My pace quickened. Having left the track, each step became a chore, the pebbles beneath my shoes slipping backwards as I pressed forward. When I reached the stone-built shelter, I noted it was in good condition, other than having no door, but I had also seen a stone wall partly surrounding an altar. *The chapel!* Not a chapel such as I would have imagined, but still a place to pray. My heart began to pound, and I battled the shingle to reach it, grateful to be able to sink to my knees before the altar and thank the Lord for this place where Avery had found shelter.

"Reverend Kenelm?"

I turned and struggled to my feet. "Avery!"

"What brings you here?" he asked, confusion on his face. "I can't offer you a drink or..."

"I had an idea," I began. "Or at least John Shearer did."

"John Shearer?"

"One of my parishioners," I explained. "He said I should come to see you."

"I can't offer you a chair, but we could sit on the stones over there and look out to sea," Avery suggested. "Then you can tell me. Although I have to say I never expected to see you again."

"Are you planning to stay here?" I asked.

"I have no plans beyond the next few days," he said, as we walked slowly towards the point where the shingle dropped away to the sea, "but I've been made welcome here. They have this beacon to tend, you see..." He gestured towards a pile of ash and part burnt wood. "I stay up through the night, keeping it burning. In return, women from the farms bring me food. It is a fair exchange and suits us all."

"Who usually watches the fire?" I asked.

"The farmers and their labourers," he told me. "There is no one else. It is not so bad in the summer when the nights are short, but they struggle in the winter and there are times when there is no way of keeping it lit. You cannot imagine how the winds howl over this place. In fact, I cannot imagine it, having only been here during fair weather."

We had sat on the shingle while Avery spoke, and a vast bay of sparkling blue-grey sea stretched out before us. Reflecting on what he told me, I watched the tide roll in, then pull back, carrying tumbling stones in the waves. "Where does the fuel come from? The wood?"

"Some from shipwrecks, some from the holly trees growing someplace over there." He waved towards the north-west. "Mostly they take a delivery by boat. It comes from the Weald, downriver to the coast and along to the beach here. They use the hermitage as a wood store, but I have made room for my bed."

I considered this, trying to picture the constant feeding of a beacon and wondering how many nights a year it was impossible to keep it burning.

Avery must have read my thoughts as he said, "It is during the stormiest nights, when the fire cannot be kept alight, that ships are wrecked here. For the sailors, there is little chance of survival. I pray for their souls." He glanced back towards the chapel.

His words took me neatly to the reason for me being there. "My curate is dead," I stated. Then, aware of how abrupt my words sounded, "He has been ill for some time and unable to assist me, but I am still saddened by his passing."

"He was an older man," Avery said. "We met at Midley."

"He was. He lived to a good age, God rest his soul."

"Is that why you came?" Avery asked. "You need an assistant, a curate, and you wondered if…"

"If you still had a vocation?" I interrupted. "Now I'm here, I don't need to ask. I can see it for myself when you speak of the chapel."

He stood, stones scattering down the bank towards the incoming tide, and I did the same.

"These past few days have given me time to think," he said. "My wife has been gone for almost a year, and I realise that it is time for me to start living amongst people again. I've had some company in my time here and could get used to it!"

I considered this as we gazed towards the horizon, and for a while we stood in companionable silence, then I asked, "Don't they mind?" I paused and considered my next words. "Don't they mind that you have been… have been with the plague victims?"

"I didn't tell them. They don't ask about my past life here."

Once more I digested his words before suggesting, "If you'd like to come to Old Romney to help with my duties, then I'd be pleased to have you. More than pleased – I could do with a young man about the place. My parish is small but Midley, as you know, stretches all the way to the Sussex border. Do you ride? There are farms and families who have been sadly neglected, and I want to make amends. If you agree, then I suggest you wait here a couple of weeks, so my people know you have been free of the plague for some time. Then stay with me – I have a spare bedroom – and we'll look out for a small cottage for you." I paused, aware he'd been given no opportunity to reply.

"Thank you. Your offer of a home and work is one I would be foolish to refuse." He looked directly at me and smiled. "Aye, I can ride and would gladly visit the outlying farms. You are right that I should remain here for a little longer but, even then, it may take a while before I'm accepted."

"They will become used to you before too long," I told him as I pictured introducing him to the people of Old Romney.

We spoke for a bit longer, mostly about parish life, but I found myself looking inland rather than out to sea. It was time for me to collect the gelding and hasten to Old Romney in time for Evensong.

When I left, we agreed Avery would stay at Denge for a couple of weeks, then join me at the rectory.

My stomach grumbled as I headed through Lydd and along the country lanes near the church at Midley. *No wonder when so many hours have passed since eating Goodwife Shearer's buns. Hopefully I'll be back at the rectory with time to eat my dinner before church.* I smiled to think of sweet Mary who would be all eagerness to heat and serve my food as soon as she saw me.

How willing she was when we shared our affectionate moment. How good of her to comfort me when I felt lost. Dear, gentle Mary... In my thoughts I was back in the parlour, and my heart began to pound as I remembered the unexpected passion. *Should I be surprised? She is a pretty thing with a lot of sense in her head.*

Might it happen again? Should it happen again? I passed Midley without even seeing the doomed church, so absorbed was I with my memories. *It would do no harm, and she seems as eager as me.* A conflicting thought came into my head. It seemed as if an angel sat on my shoulder and spoke wise words: *Loving she may be, but Mary is young and naïve. She has some education but has travelled no further than New Romney. Be gentle if you are growing to love her. If not, leave her be.*

"Oh! There is no need to speak of love when I am newly widowed. Let us think of companionship and affection," I replied aloud. With this, I urged the chestnut to canter, and the angel was swept from my shoulder.

On arriving back home in Old Romney, I spotted a lad in the lane, dismounted and handed him the reins. "Take this horse back to John Shearer, will you? He needs rubbing down, food and water. We have travelled for several miles."

The lad nodded and mumbled his response.

"Oh, and tell John that my quest was a success. Tomorrow, come to my kitchen door and Goodwife Beth will give you a basket of food."

He grinned. "Thank you, sir. I'll take care of the horse and be grateful for the food. Thank you kindly."

I entered a silent house and stood in the hallway listening. It was rare not to hear the clatter of a pan, the movement of a chair. Walking into the kitchen, I found Mary sitting slumped forward on the table, golden hair tumbling onto the scrubbed table, covering her features.

"Mary! Dear God, what has happened?" I asked, my voice gentle.

She lifted a tear-stained face and stared at me, "Oh, it's nothing. Nothing at all." Then her eyes filled with tears and slowly overfilled. She made no fuss at all, but merely said, "Will you be wanting your dinner? I can warm it through, but it won't be as tasty as it was… as it was earlier."

"Thank you," I replied. "I've been for a long ride. If this water is warm," I glanced towards the kettle hanging over the fire, "then I'll have a wash first."

"I'll carry it up for you," she said, while looking about the place for something.

Then it came to me that she needed a handkerchief, and I happened to have a clean one in my pocket. I passed it to her, and she took it, then turned away to wipe her face. There was no reason for me to stay but she still looked so vulnerable and so… so tempting. I stepped forward, wrapping both arms around her, leaning in to nuzzle her neck and, as she turned, my kisses moved to the soft white flesh exposed above the lace of her shift. She murmured her surprise, and I silenced her with my lips on hers. I knew my kiss to be savage. Unrestrained. The trip to the coast… the hours on horseback… they had not wearied me but given me a zest for new adventures. At that moment, there seemed no better place to be than in the arms of my sweet Mary. My lust for her felt all consuming, but a rap on the open back door brought me to my senses. I removed my hand from under her skirt, stepping back as someone entered the kitchen.

Mary fled from the room, and I turned to face Goodwife Beth.

"You're back then, sir."

"Did you want something?" I asked as if she had interrupted no more than a passing conversation between me and the maid.

"Only to see that all was well. She was so upset, Mary was. I keep an eye on her, what with her mother being gone these past four years. Dinner was ready and you nowhere to be found. But you're back now..."

"I'm back. Parish business..." I excused myself. "Mary is just taking hot water up to my room."

I saw her narrowed eyes look to the kettle still hanging over the fire. She said nothing.

"I'll see you tomorrow then." I smiled – at least my lips curved in a smile.

Now I understood the reason for Mary's tears. I should not have needed Goodwife Beth to put me straight.

"Do you enjoy working here for me?" I asked, when she remained standing on the threshold.

"It suits me well," she replied, not answering my question.

"You're not a gossip, Beth. I like that about you."

"I'm not a gossip, sir." With this she turned and walked away.

I stood in the centre of the room, looking towards the open doorway, not knowing who to curse first. Mary for tempting me, Goodwife Beth for her motherly instincts or myself for succumbing to my desires in the kitchen.

Unsure of where Mary cowered, I took the kettle upstairs and busied myself with washing away the sweat and dust from the ride to Denge. When I returned to the kitchen, Mary had re-heated my dinner; she gave me a slight nod and carried the plate to the parlour, brushing against me as she passed.

"Thank you," I said, following her. "Mary, there's something I have to tell you."

She looked at me, her expression both curious and worried.

"We are to have a new curate – a young man."

"A new one… a new curate already!" her voice rose with surprise. She paused to consider it. "A young man, you say. That will be such a help."

"I've neglected this parish and Midley for long enough and mean to remedy it." She did not reply to this but stood gazing at me while I lifted my cutlery and speared some meat with my fork. "The second bedroom must be prepared for him. You'll know what to do and you have two weeks."

"Oh! Of course, sir. He's to live here. I hadn't thought…"

"He'll be here for a month, six weeks perhaps," I explained before taking my first mouthful. "He'll have his own place eventually."

Sweet Mary dipped a small curtsey and left.

My curate, Avery, will be living here in the house, his eyes open to everything. This will please the angel on my shoulder who tells me to be gentle with Mary. The angel says I should consider Mary carefully – lovely as she is, could she be the next Mistress Kenelm? The devil sits on my other shoulder and interrupts the angel, telling me that I can send the curate to the outer reaches of Midley, safe in the knowledge that he will be away for some hours. The devil makes me smile and think of my Mary's loving response to my growing passion.

Mary

One moment I am so happy, the next I wallow in despair. Goodwife Beth gives me stern looks and shakes her head. The rector is both kindly and uncaring, so I can make no sense of his feelings towards me. Let me start at the beginning.

Yesterday, my rector did not come home after church. I had seen him after the service, and he told me that he had no plans to go to Midley. When he didn't return for dinner, I went to his wife's grave and then looked inside the church. He could not be found. Back to the rectory I went, expecting to find him there, but no luck. I walked along Five Vents Lane, then a short way along the old lane to New Romney, then in the other direction towards Midley. Hot and thirsty, I retreated to the rectory where I ate my dinner and left the rector's meal on a covered plate.

All afternoon, I struggled to settle to anything. My patchwork was picked up and put down a dozen times, and the same with my darning. I went to the upstairs windows again and again but could see no sign of him. In the end I could bear it no more and, certain something awful had happened, I sobbed at the table. Goodwife Beth came, despite its being her day off, and sat with me for a while. She didn't understand why I felt so worried, but we had met in the lane when I was looking for the rector, and she had seen I was distressed.

Just when I was beginning to think he would not return for Evensong, Reverend Kenelm strode in, looking as if he had been on some great adventure and had stories to share. I don't know how it happened, but he was so sad to have upset me and must have thought it the best way to comfort me: he held me, and we kissed, right there in the kitchen.

How foolish – there's no privacy in the rectory kitchen. Beth walked in, and I ran away – up the stairs to the attic. I don't know what happened next, down there in the kitchen, but she knows now – Beth knows my rector cares very much for me. At least, she *should* understand his affection for me, but she is intent on being cruel.

"I saw you with him," she hissed while wrapping an apron around her scrawny body this morning. "How long has it been going on?"

"A few days," I whispered. We kept our voices low because my rector was in the parlour and the doors were open to allow a summer breeze to flow through the house. "Please don't tell anyone."

"I won't tell anyone. I won't cast shame on the memory of your parents," she replied, removing a pan from a hook and slamming it on the table.

"There's no shame," I answered. *Shame* – the word rattled about in my mind. "He's been widowed for more than six months. Isn't that enough?"

Beth didn't answer this, but continued, "I thought – the whole village thought – it was the coming of the archbishop that had perked him up. But it was a kiss and a cuddle with the maid that put the smile on his face."

"It *was* the archbishop!" I protested. "It was. Then he wanted to show me how grateful he was for all my help."

"Grateful!" she scoffed. "A shilling to spend in New Romney or a length of ribbon would have done. What do you think will become of you now?"

I couldn't answer because we heard the scrape of a chair and the rector's footsteps. "Have you heard?" he asked, appearing at the kitchen doorway. "There are to be some changes here."

I glanced at Beth and saw the disbelief flash across her face. *She thinks he is talking about me and him.* I smiled to see her caught out.

"We are to have a new curate," Reverend Kenelm continued. "He'll be living here for a while, so there will be a little more work for both of you."

"A curate!" Beth squeaked. "That will make a change. It's no trouble to feed an extra mouth and, sir, if you don't mind my saying, I'm pleased to think of you having the company as well as help in the parish."

"Thank you, Beth." The rector gave a broad smile. "Of course, I'll be thinking about marrying again one day, and you'll have another mistress here. For now, we will concentrate on Mister Bridgeman who will be with us in a couple of weeks. Mary, if you need any help with heavy work upstairs, then ask the lad. I'm sure you'll find him willing."

With this, Beth and I were left on our own again. She remained speechless for some time, no doubt stunned to hear of the rector speaking so openly about his plans. I continued with my chores, a smile on my face and a skip in my step.

The second bedroom had remained untouched since the mistress and the baby died. I suspect my rector had given no thought to the packages of swaddling bands, bonnets, shawls and tiny sheets of hemmed linen. *Best not mention these to him.* I bundled them into my arms and took them up to store in the low attic room. *He'll ask about them one day, but no need to remind him now.* The room had a small window, and the morning light shone on a wooden crib. I gazed at it. Already, cobwebs were gathering dust and dead flies lay in one corner. With my heart feeling heavy, I left the attic, carefully descending the steep, narrow stairs, and returned to the main part of the home where everything was familiar and in order.

The bedroom, with its bed, trunk and clothes press, was now empty of possessions and soon cleaned. "It will just need a quick polish and sweep on the day he arrives," I told Beth.

"The sooner the better," she replied.

"Two weeks," I reminded her.

"Two weeks too long," she muttered while kneading bread. "When he's here, the rector will have another man to speak to about parish business and that will put a stop to your cosy chats."

"We'll just have to see…" I replied before heading out to collect eggs.

Later, when her chores were completed and Beth prepared to return to her own home, she suggested. "Why don't you ask if you can have the attic room? No need to sleep down here in little more than a cupboard. It won't be wrong if there's two of them in the house."

I had always liked the idea of having a proper room, rather than sleeping off the kitchen. But now I thought of the empty crib and shuddered. "Oh, I don't know. Maybe…"

"I hope you're not harbouring thoughts of making your bed with him…" Beth muttered, a dark look on her face.

"Oh! I…" Turning towards the fire, I stirred the stew.

"I hope I'm wrong about your intentions, Mary. You always were the sensible sister – don't forget that." With this, Beth left the rectory, and I was glad. There had never been any bad feeling between us before and it had made me feel miserable all morning.

After his dinner, my rector reached out, placing a hand on my arm as I went to take his plate away. "Mary, we have the curate coming to live here soon."

"We do, sir."

"Thank you for cleaning the bedroom."

"You're welcome." I should have moved away then, but his fingers on my arm were comforting.

"I expect it's rather a mess in the attic, but it makes a nice enough room. I believe there's an old bed up there."

How strange that he should mention it so soon after Beth's departing words. "Were you thinking of the curate sleeping up there?" I asked. "The room could be cleaned up, but if he's a tall man, it may not suit him."

"Not the curate. I was thinking of you, sleeping in that... well, it can't be called a room, can it? Things are changing here, and I wondered if the attic would suit you better?"

I considered his words, pushing the thought of the crib aside and, instead, remembering the view from the small window and the space available if the trunks and old furniture were pushed into the lowest space under the eaves. "It would take some work, sir, but if you think it best... If you think it more proper."

"That's exactly what I think, sweet Mary."

I could think of nothing more to say. All I could do was gaze at him and thank the Lord for my good fortune. It would take a while to clear and clean the attic room, and maybe hem some new curtains for the window, but this was my path to a better place. *I must be there in the attic by the time the curate comes. What respect will he have for me and my rector if he sees me sleeping in the kitchen? He will think better of us both if I am in the attic when he realises that the rector and I are to marry.*

Avery

Today I put Denge behind me and walked to Old Romney to start a new chapter in my life. It only felt right that I made a slight diversion to see Midley church. Nothing had changed, other than it seemed more tired than it had only three weeks ago, if that were possible. How strange to think that, as curate, this church and the people of this parish will be part of my duties – if Archbishop Parker thinks the church worth saving.

After the weeks of living by the coast, with a shingle landscape as far as the eye could see, I soon noticed the change of season across the pasture and cultivated fields. Crops had been harvested, their stubble remaining, and the lambs were stockier. There was something else – something subtle – a weariness in the long grasses, crispy edges to the leaves, and the feathery reed tops had scattered in the breeze. Summer was moving into autumn and, although there would be many warm days to come over the next weeks, this day reminded me of that shift in the seasons.

On my way, I cowered under holm oaks in Lydd when an abrupt shower had the townsfolk running for shelter, but was caught in the open as I approached Old Romney. By the time I reached the village, my jerkin and shirt were damp across the shoulders, my hose were mud-splattered, and I looked like a travelling pedlar. In my time at Denge, they thought nothing of me being a little ragged. Before that, as body washer, I had no need to worry about a tattered hem or cuff, although I always did my best to stay clean – I owed the dead that. *There is nothing to be done but ask the rector's advice. Only a year ago, these clothes were good enough for a curate and some can be repaired.*

I passed villagers without receiving any curious glances and realised I may have tended their dead, but few had looked directly at me. I had been invisible. *It will only take one to recognise you and they will all know.* I shrugged the thoughts away, knowing there was nothing to be done but wait for their unease to pass.

At the rectory I faltered. *Front door or kitchen? It must be the front.* I strode up and gave a confident rap. A young woman answered, "Hello... Good afternoon, I mean. Are you? You must be..."

"I'm the new curate, Avery Bridgeman."

"Pleased to meet you, sir. I'm Mary."

With her pleasant voice, clear skin and blonde hair pulled back into a neat bun, I liked the look of

Mary immediately. She wore an apron, so I assumed she worked for Reverend Edward Kenelm, but she could have been a relation.

"The rector is in the garden giving instructions to the boy who works for us," she told me. "If you don't mind waiting in here, I'll fetch him immediately."

I was left in a neat, square parlour with a small dining table and a couple of easy chairs. Tapestries and amateur oil paintings adorned the walls, and I studied them rather than sit and wait. Mary had spoken of the boy who works for 'us', giving me a clue that she was confident in her position at the rectory, but I knew she was not the rector's wife – he had told me he was widowed. *Most likely a family member,* I decided.

The day passed quickly after that. We men spoke over wine and spiced cake at the parlour table, fussed over by Mary. Then the rector took me to my bedroom, directly over his study, with views across the fields towards the plague pits (not that I could see them from there) and to the village called Hope which I could see. He presented me with a set of clean clothes, saying they had belonged to the previous curate. Mine could be washed and mended, but he suggested a trip to New Romney so I could be measured and fitted for a new outfit.

"We have something in common, you and I," Reverend Kenelm said when we strolled around the churchyard.

I knew he referred to the deaths of our wives.

"We do, sir."

"I'll not forget, but the dark days have passed, and I look forward to serving my parish better."

"I do not forget either," I replied. "But it is time to stop living as a recluse and I thank you for welcoming me here." I knew neither of us wanted to linger on that subject, so I asked, "Has there been any news from Archbishop Parker?"

"Nothing, but I hope to hear from him soon."

Then we entered the church – a plain, solid place. I couldn't help comparing it to St Peter and St Paul at Newchurch, which was far more spacious, and then with the little place at Midley, which was much smaller. I knew at once that within these walls people had felt much sadness and suffering, but the ancient stones and wooden beams offered a healing presence. Breathing deeply, I inhaled the scents of candlewax and burning wicks, the slight dampness of the ragstone and the richness of polish on gleaming tables and benches. Without exchanging any words with the rector, I walked along the nave to the chancel and knelt before the altar, giving thanks to the Lord.

It has been eight months since I slept in a bed, and it will feel strange at first. As I lie here, I can hear the creaking of the attic floorboards above me and, outside, the distant hoot of an owl, clicking of bats and the creak of a gate or bough. I believe I will be made welcome by the people of Old Romney and those living and working at the rectory.

Mary sleeps in the attic room, but I am none the wiser as to who she is. The rector treats her with kindness and, I think, affection. When encouraged to speak to me, I found out that she could read and write, and she hinted at time spent encouraging the grieving rector to write his sermons. Sometimes, I wonder if she is to be the next Mistress Kenelm, but the next moment I realise that his future wife would not eat alone at the kitchen table.

He would do well to marry her. Any man would do well to marry her. Perhaps I have it all wrong – she could be a relation and neither has thought to mention it to me. As I drift in and out of sleep, I think that is more likely. There has been talk of a cook who comes to the rectory every morning. I have decided that I will see how the cook treats Mary and that will help me decide exactly what her role is within this seemingly happy home.

Mary

At the rectory, we have settled into new patterns now there is both my rector and Mister Bridgeman to look after. Reverend Kenelm has said that if there is too much work for me, I can find a girl from the village to help, perhaps with the laundry. For now, I am determined to show how well I can manage. After all, the curate will not live with us for long, and our lives will change again when he is settled in a cottage.

In the kitchen, Goodwife Beth and I busy ourselves with preserving fruit and vegetables for the harsh winter months ahead. "I'll stay a little longer today," Beth says most mornings. "If we can bottle this now, we'll be thankful later on." We are determined that the larder shelves will be filled with jars of pickled vegetables and jams from summer fruits.

Outside, the apples and pears from the orchard are being gathered by the lad who works in the garden and by Mister Bridgeman who is eager to help. They are placing the fruit on boards set on the rafters in the small barn where we keep tools and firewood, and I hear the curate speaking about how he will keep his eye on the fruit in case any bruises begin to form. "Once there is a bruise, there will be rot within days," he tells us solemnly. "Within a week all the fruit around will have rotten."

I feel content and at peace with my life. My rector is humming to himself as he sits at his desk or moves about the home, and it must be because he is happy again. He has a young, enthusiastic curate to help within this parish and Midley, and can carry with him the memories of our sweet kisses. Of course, this newcomer in the home means that the rector and I cannot spend as much time alone together as we would like. However, it has been decided that Mister Bridgeman will ride to Midley two or three times a week so all the men and women living in the outlying farms and cottages know that they are no longer abandoned by Reverend Kenelm and that they are just as important as those living here in Old Romney.

In the afternoons, while the curate is away and when Beth has returned to her own home, my rector and I slip into our old ways, with me listening to his ideas for sermons or sharing snippets of news I pick up both here and in New Romney. "Why not call me Edward," he has said, "when it is just you and I?"

As September draws to a close, we have been awaiting the news from Canterbury and cannot help wondering if the archbishop is understanding about the troubles faced by a lone rector running the two parishes. At last, the news has come.

A rap came at the part-open kitchen door today. A young man stood there, his shirt and breeches soiled, his brow glistening, and a merry smile on his face. "Letter for Reverend Kenelm," he announced.

I had been eating my dinner at the kitchen table and quickly rose to meet him at the door. "From Canterbury?" I asked, reaching for the envelope.

"That's the rector's business," he told me, moving it away from my grasp. "Give me a kiss and I'll tell you."

"I don't go giving out kisses," I replied, scowling. "But I can tell the rector you're here and causing bother."

"How about a beaker of ale then?" he conceded, handing me the letter. "It's from Canterbury."

"All right, but you can sit on that bench outside."

I kept an eye on him while he guzzled the ale, and took the letter through to my rector once the lad was on his way. He seemed absorbed with his thoughts but turned from his desk and smiled as I knocked and entered the small room where he worked.

"Sir... There's a letter come... From Canterbury, he said."

"It's here then."

"It's here." I gave a small smile and backed away.

I couldn't settle to anything after that. With an eye on the swill bin, I ate my dinner, knowing I should not be wasteful. Then I tidied the kitchen and flitted between the garden and kitchen, feeling surer with each moment that passed that the news must be bad.

Eventually, I decided to fetch my patchwork and try to settle to hemming some squares. I went to my attic room, hoping to hear something from Edward, but nothing... On my return, he called, "Mary, is that you?"

My heart swelled. *Whatever the news, he chooses to share it with me!*

"It is!"

"Come in then. I have news from the archbishop."

He sounded cheerful enough, so I opened the door to find my rector standing by his desk, the open letter in his hand. He stepped towards the window to illuminate the words, and I gazed at him expectantly.

"I hardly know how to say it," he began. "Midley is finished, as I suspected, and I cannot bring myself to feel too bad about it. St Clement's is saved, but my prolonged period of mourning has led to a lack of faith in me. Let me start with Midley..."

"A lack of faith?" I could not help interrupting. Reaching forward I took his free hand. "Doesn't he see that you are so much better?"

"He sees it, so it is not all bad. But let us start with Midley: he describes the place as 'greatly decayed, the windows unglazed, floor tiles lifted, and the church not fit for serving God'."

"He is right," I murmured.

"The church, he says 'lacks the necessary books'. I cannot think where they have gone, but they could not be found when we went there. Perhaps they were so decayed that our late curate took his own copies when he went there. I cannot ask him now. But there is something else, Mary. He states that someone from Deanes Farm – over Brookland way – has taken and sold the church goods!"

"Deanes Farm?" I exclaimed, "But…"

My rector seemed to barely hear me, and continued, "It is clear from this whole report that Archbishop Parker did not merely visit each church but took it upon himself to speak with the people he met on the way. How else could he discover such things?"

"He must have…" I agreed. "You said Deanes Farm and that is where my sister, Lucy, lives, or rather lived, as we are certain she is dead."

At this he paused, and his grey eyes gazed at me with a tenderness I had not seen before. "We must find out, sweet Mary." Then his tone changed, and he blurted out, "How odd that she should be at the same place. He was seen, the farmer, looting the place! But how it is known that he sold the church plate and other valuables, I cannot say. There must be someone left at the farm and perhaps they would know."

"There must be someone left," I echoed. "What is to become of the church?"

"It will be left to ruin. If there were a private house nearby, perhaps they would keep it as their chapel, but that is not to be. I'll speak to Avery, and we can fix up a sign – if men want to use the stone and wood, they should ask me. The walls and timber will be of value to someone, and some extra shillings will help keep St Clement's in better repair."

Left to ruin. Here in Old Romney two ruined churches now give shelter to sheep, and stone by stone they are reused. I found my thoughts drifting, but Edward continued speaking, bringing me back to the present.

"St Clement's, as I said, is saved. Our parish is small, but the church well attended. People have spoken against me, dear Mary, and told of me not wearing a surplice for the service."

"You do now, sir."

"I do and it is all thanks to you that I was well-presented when Archbishop Parker visited. I am surprised he mentioned it in his report, but that is done, and I have my Mary to tend to my hems and collars and keep me in order."

"You do, sir. And the church?"

"Thankfully, the roof had been repaired, and he saw no great fault in the building. I told him that there has been a bequest – half to the church and half to the poor – and this pleased him."

At that moment, footsteps could be heard approaching from the kitchen. I stepped back and into the shadows of the room.

"Avery! The letter has come. Let me tell you about it over a glass of something." Reverend Kenelm beamed at the new curate and waved the letter in his direction as I slipped from the room and into the kitchen.

As I drift into sleep, my thoughts take me across the fields to Midley. I wonder who built the church there and am thankful that they cannot see how it is left to ruin. My mother used to say that our family came from Midley, some generations before, and had connections with the first farm there. It is just a story - we have no record of it, only what is passed down through word of mouth. Ma told me once that she called me and my sisters plain, sensible names, but sometimes she wished she had been bold enough to name me after one of my female ancestors – Juliana or Gisella. "I suit a plain name," I remember saying. Now, in this dreamy state, I wonder if my rector would prefer to take Juliana or Gisella as his next wife, rather than ordinary Mary. Through the floorboards, I hear him move in his bed and I wonder...

Mary

"What were you doing sitting near the front?" Kitty asked as we met outside the porch at St Clement's. My sister is like that – saying what she thinks without any friendly greeting first.

"Hello Kitty, how are you?" I asked, ignoring her question.

"We're having a new floor at Wheelsgate," she told me. "It will be easier to keep clean. You don't know how lucky you are, not having dirt floors over there." She jerked her head in the direction of the rectory.

I wandered in the direction of our parents' graves, and she followed. "I'm glad you're settled there," I said. "Glad you're treated well."

Although Kitty comes to church most Sundays, I don't always have the chance to speak to her. Whereas I always go to the morning service and sometimes the evening one, she usually attends the evening service, missing the early one as she is needed at Wheelsgate to make the dinner for the family. If she can stop and chat for a moment, then she is just as keen to speak to old friends and neighbours as her sister. Recently, a young man called Jack has been distracting her.

It had been several weeks since we last spoke of Lucy and I was eager to know if Kitty had any news of her. "Have you seen Lucy," I asked. "Has she started visiting again after church?"

"I haven't seen her since her master had the..." Kitty lowered her voice, "You know... since he died."

"But that was before the summer! And she's not been back since?"

"She's not been back." Kitty, who usually had so much to say, paused for a moment. "When did you see her?"

"Before all this business with the archbishop. July, I think."

"It's not like Lucy, is it? She used to come along to Wheelsgate every week if the weather was fair."

We stood in silence for a while, both of us gazing down at the graves with their wooden crosses and both not wanting to voice our thoughts. I raised my head and looked towards the village called Hope.

"I'll ask Reverend Kenelm if I can go to Deanes Farm," I said eventually. "Even if she's... if she's gone, then someone will know. Or maybe she's got a new master and mistress, and they won't let her come and see us. That could be it."

"It could be," Kitty replied, but I could hear the doubt in her voice.

"I'll walk down the lane with you," I suggested, knowing that Kitty couldn't linger.

"And you can tell me why you're not sitting at the back anymore," my sister persisted.

I considered my answer before saying, "He said… the rector said that I'm so helpful and should not be sitting back there. Mister Bridgeman agreed."

"The body washer?"

Why must she always be so harsh? I scowled and looked around, but no one had come to this part of the graveyard. "We don't say that now, Kitty. He's a curate and properly trained. Mister Bridgeman is a good man and treats me kindly."

She shrugged. "If you're going to walk with me for a bit, we had better get going. I'm surprised, that's all. Surprised about him being a curate and you sitting halfway down the nave."

"Well, it's good to have a surprise!" I grinned, pleased with myself.

But Kitty could not help harping on, liking to put me and Lucy in our places. "I don't know what the rector is thinking of. It's maids at the back with the labourers – always has been. I bet our Lucy knew to go to the back of the church."

"Knew!" I cried out. "Don't you dare say it like that. Don't you say it like she's gone before we know."

"It's what we think," she countered. "You ask the rector if you can go over and find out. But if you see her, then you can tell her from me that I'm upset that she hasn't bothered to come over to Wheelsgate. I can't go trekking out to Brookland – the mistress won't let me."

"I'll ask him later."

Nothing I said or did could please my sister today. "Halfway down the nave," she muttered. "You're the same as me, Mary. Same as me and Lucy – just a maid."

"You're wrong, Kitty," I blurted. "I'm in charge of the rectory and the rector would tell you the same thing if you asked."

"Maybe I will!"

With this we parted, and I scurried back to the rectory – it wouldn't do to keep the men waiting for their dinner.

"Can you spare a moment?" I asked my rector after they had finished eating and I hovered at the doorway with a tray of their dirty plates and cutlery. "After I've done the dishes, or…?"

Edward nodded, setting aside his napkin. "Of course, Mary. What is it?"

Avery stood, his chair scraping on the stone floor.

"Mister Bridgeman, I don't mind… It's not private," Then I hesitated, feeling the weight of my concern for Lucy, as both men looked at me. "It's about Lucy, my younger sister. Kitty is worried, and so am I. We haven't heard from her, and we don't know if she's still there at Deanes Farm. Her master and mistress both went to the pit, but we don't know about Lucy. I'd like to go there and find if she's kept at home by a new master or gone elsewhere. Someone must know."

My rector regarded me thoughtfully. "Lucy has always been a reliable girl. If she hasn't returned or sent word, there must be a reason." He paused, turning to Mister Bridgeman, "Avery, do you know this young woman?"

"Deanes Farm?" the curate said. "I've been there twice, and I saw the girl, but never went to tend to her body. I didn't realise she was your sister, Mary, and I can't tell you any more."

"Then you must go, and as soon as possible." Edward stood, indicating the matter was dealt with.

"Thank you, sir," I said, feeling a surge of hope. "If it suits Goodwife Beth, then I'll go there tomorrow."

As I turned to leave, Edward's voice stopped me. "Mary, if Lucy is there and needs assistance, please bring her back with you. She can make her home here while it suits her, and she will be among familiar faces."

I nodded, grateful for his understanding and support. "I will, sir. Thank you."

With that, I left the room, my mind already racing with plans, hopeful of finding Lucy alive.

Lucy

While a pan of mutton stew simmered over the fire, it came to mind that I should cut the lavender growing in thick bushes either side of our front gate. So, there I was, with a trug at my feet and a knife to hand, busy with my task, when something made me pause and look. When I saw a woman approaching, I didn't recognise her at first. So few women walk along our lane, and I stepped through the gateway to see if she needed any help.

"Lucy! Oh, my goodness. It's you!" the woman cried, and I thought it rather odd, but then I realised...

"Mary! You've come to see me! Have you really come to see me?" Foolish words maybe, but it's what I said.

"I have! We hadn't seen you – not me, nor Kitty. I had to come." She reached out, taking my hands and studying me. "I've never seen you looking so well. What's happened, Lucy? Do you have a new master and mistress? Do they treat you kindly?"

I smiled and pulled Mary towards the farmhouse, picking up the trug on the way. "I'm the new mistress

– can you believe it? It's my farm now – mine and Davey's."

"Davey?" she repeated. At that moment, Mary must have felt my wedding band as her fingers were clasped over mine. She moved her hand so only the tips of my fingers were in hers and the gold ring revealed. "Oh, my goodness, Lucy," she whispered. "You're the first of us to marry. Why didn't you say?"

"I was just busy being married," I told her.

"Too busy to tell your sisters you were still alive?" she asked, her words wobbling. "Didn't you realise… didn't you think that we believed you had died?"

I had been feeling so smug – so proud – that to see Mary openly crying made me cry too.

"I'm sorry," I babbled. "Kitty was so horrible. She's always nasty to me, but there was no excuse not to tell you. It's all been wonderful, with Davey's ma treating me so kindly, and he has brothers here in Brookland who we see on a Sunday, and I couldn't bear to go and see Kitty and have her find fault in me." I paused and flung my arms around Mary. "I'm sorry, Mary. I truly am. What will Davey think when he sees what a cruel sister I am?"

Mary mopped up her tears, and mine too. We walked into the farmhouse with our arms linked. "Sit here at the table." I gestured to one of three chairs, then fetched clay mugs and picked a sprig of rosemary from a bundle. Having poured hot water over the herb, I sat opposite Mary, ready to share my news.

"The master and the mistress died, but you know that," I began, my thoughts taking me to those days when our skin reeked of Four Thieves and the air of smouldering herbs. "Then it was just me and Davey. We stayed here, knowing to keep away from the village."

Mary nodded and her brow creased, but she said nothing.

"Then one day Davey told me that Mister Walter had said he, Davey, could have the farm. There was no family, you see. We knew we had been lucky to escape the plague, and Davey said we should marry." I couldn't help myself from smiling, even though Mary sat there looking so worried. "I had never thought about being married, but Davey was always friendly and thoughtful, so it seemed like a good idea."

"Was it a good idea?" Mary asked.

"It was! We set up home here. Think of that, Mary, me having my own room – up there where they used to be. Now it's me and my husband who are master and mistress of the place. He's so kind to me, and there's none of the shouting that I used to hear about the place. We go to church on Sunday, and now I can sit with all his family. Halfway down the aisle, we are! There's a young man working for us, but I don't have a maid. I'll have one soon though!" With those last words, I could hardly keep the triumph from my voice.

"I'm so happy for you, Lucy," Mary began, her beautiful blue eyes filling with tears again. "But don't you see how worried I was? How did you escape the plague? We thought you had…"

"I used the Four Thieves, but I think…" I paused, wondering how to put my thoughts into words. "I think God chose to spare me and Davey. Like that man who washed the bodies. He's been spared over and over, hasn't he?"

My sister beamed, and I knew she had some great story to tell. I realised she had felt cross with me, but now we were both friends and sisters once more.

"He's not a body washer now," Mary started. For a moment she reminded me of our dear mother, and I felt that I was back at the fireside with Ma and my two sisters. Mary told the story well, and I drank in the details of the wandering curate-cum-body washer. All the time we talked, the mutton stew bubbled over the fire.

Footsteps and the call of one man to the other reminded me of my duties. Davey and Robert were back for their dinner, and there was I sitting about gossiping. I jumped up. "Mary, you'll stay to eat with us, won't you?" Before she could answer, the men stepped into the kitchen, their talk cut abruptly by the surprise at seeing another woman with me. "This is my sister, Mary, come to visit from Old Romney," I told them.

I stepped towards Davey, my tall gentle husband, and he placed his arm around my waist as he greeted Mary. "I'm so pleased you were able to come to see us. Lucy has met all my family, and I have seen none of hers."

"It's only me and Kitty, but I'm pleased to meet you," Mary responded, "and to find Lucy so well settled." She glanced at Robert, the young farmhand whose face had been so badly scarred by the plague.

"This is Robert," Davey said. "We work this place together."

"I'm pleased to meet you both," Mary answered in her gentle way.

It only took a moment to ladle stew into dishes and, while I busied myself, I couldn't help looking back at Davey and notice how kindly he spoke to Mary and how she smiled as she told him a little about her life in Old Romney. I thought back to that day when Davey said we should marry. I hadn't known how lucky I was, but I knew now.

We lingered over our meal, despite all the work to be done on the fields. News was shared between us and opinions exchanged. Then Mary said that she should help me tidy up before going home. "I must leave soon," she said. "The rector will be expecting me."

"Mary, if you ever find that life doesn't suit you at the rectory, then there is a place for you here," Davey told her as he and Robert went to leave. "You have a brother now and one who would be glad to give you a home."

I smiled at Davey, once more thankful for my good fortune, then looked expectantly at Mary.

"I'm grateful and pleased to call you my brother," Mary replied, "but I'm settled at the rectory."

I eyed the space under the stairs where I used to sleep on a pallet. Mary followed my gaze, and I think she knew that, if she came to us, she would have no space to call her own.

"I've got my attic room all to myself," she added. "The rector is kind and Mister Bridgeman, the curate, is good to me."

"You're settled of course," Davey agreed. "I'm glad for you. Lucy, you should go to visit your other sister, Kitty. I know she upset you, but it's time to make amends. She's welcome here too, you know."

"I will go to see her," I agreed. "It's time to be friends again, and I'd like to tell her my news." With this, the men left, leaving Mary and me to tidy up after the meal before she set off, me joining her for the first mile or so.

Walking along the lane to Brookland with Mary, we chatted about those days when we three girls lived at home with our parents. "I've been making a patchwork bedcover from Ma's scraps," Mary told me. "It's coming along nicely."

"Have you used the indigo?" I asked.

"I have. It's for the eight diamonds which come together to make a star."

I thought about Mary's patchwork and what a neat hand she had, then my thoughts turned to the bed I shared with Davey and how I had planned to make my own quilt. Suddenly, it didn't seem fair that Mary had all those scraps from Ma and I had none. It didn't seem right that I was the married sister with no patchwork.

"Davey and I are married," I stated as we neared the village. "By rights that bedcover should be ours."

"Yours?" Mary's eyes widened. "But I made it."

"Perhaps you made it as a wedding gift?" I don't know what had got into me – I coveted that quilt. I had never wanted anything fancy before, but I wanted this.

"I'm happy you're married," Mary answered. "I've never met a nicer man than your Davey, but you're not having my patchwork." Then she stopped right there in the middle of the road and turned to face me. "I'll have it on my own bed when I'm married."

"Married?" I squeaked. "You didn't say."

"I didn't say because I came to see you and hear your news."

"Who are you marrying?" I pictured my farmhouse and all our land – me and Davey, King and

Queen of it all. I had done well and prepared myself to be pleased for Mary.

"The rector. My rector!"

I frowned. Standing there on the lane with Mary, I couldn't quite understand what she was saying. Little Lucy they used to call me. Mary was the clever one. Kitty had a sharp tongue, but her wits were fast enough. I was always Little Lucy.

"You mean some man who wants to be in the Church? Some man that comes to see the rector and he's taken a liking to you. You've done well, Mary."

"I don't know about any man who comes to see the rector – it's Reverend Edward Kenelm I'll be marrying," Mary told me, her eyes shining and face alight with joy, as if she saw herself exchanging vows. "So, I'll be keeping my patchwork. Now, I need to pick up my pace or he'll be worrying about me."

With that Mary strode off down the lane, turning once to look at me and wave. I returned to my Davey – but for some reason I didn't share Mary's news straight away. I needed time to consider it first.

Kitty

"Is that your sister? The quiet one?" my mistress asked as we left Wheelsgate for church. "It's not her normal time."

I frowned, studying the familiar figure walking towards us from the direction of Brookland. "I'd say it was Mary, if she wasn't coming from the wrong way," I replied. "It must be... It must be Little Lucy!"

"Go to her then, and church can wait till later," the mistress said. "There's a story to be told and you need to hear it."

Separating from the others, I ran towards my sister. "Lucy!" I called. "Where have you been all this time?"

"Kitty!" Lucy cried out in return, "I'm sorry I've not been this way in a while."

By this time, we were in each other's arms, hugging, then separating to look at each other. For that moment, I felt so happy to hold my sister, and so surprised to see her again, that my usual frustrations with Lucy were forgotten. This sisterly love was soon broken by her next words: "I've been busy being married."

"Married?" I snapped. "You can't be married. Not before me and Mary. Who would want to marry you?" My cruel words were uttered before I had a chance to hold them in.

Lucy stepped back as if I had slapped her. "Well, that's how it is, and I can't undo it, not even for you."

"I'm sorry," I mumbled. "I was just so surprised." But no sooner had the apology passed my lips than the next wave of fury was rising. "Why didn't you tell us, Lucy? Why did you stay away?"

"I've got a home to run now. I can't just be coming over here. Besides, you were horrid last time I saw you."

"Because you came here carrying the plague," I reminded her. "Anyway, are you coming back to Wheelsgate? There's bread and milk, and the floor is coming on nicely."

We turned and walked back to the farm, filling the air with a stream of chatter about our memories of growing up in Old Romney. Then, as we entered the house by the kitchen door, I thought to ask, "Who did you marry? A farm boy?"

"Not a farmhand," Lucy replied. "Davey took on Deanes Farm from Mister Walter, so I married a farmer and I'm his wife!" She must have seen the jealousy flash across my face because she swiftly added, "It's just a small place. Not a grand farm like this. How good those tiles look. How pleased you must be."

"But it's *your* farm," I stressed.

"It is."

I busied myself with cutting yesterday's bread and fetching a dish of dripping. Finally, I poured us both a cup of creamy milk. Lucy twittered on about the floor tiles and how clean I kept them. Then, when I thought she could shock me no more, she announced, "Mary's getting married too!"

"Mary? How do you know?"

"She came to Deanes Farm two days ago and told me that she's marrying the rector over at Old Romney. You must know him, what with him being your rector too. I suppose you already knew about them getting married."

"I didn't."

"Oh!" Lucy considered this, then continued, "She's making a patchwork cover for their bed and, when it's done, they'll marry."

I didn't speak much after that. I couldn't bring myself to talk about both my sisters being married and running their own homes. Even the new floor tiles couldn't bring a smile to my face now.

Mary

The oddest thing happened when Kitty came to see me today. She arrived late morning, with a nervous grin on her face and a sparkle in her eyes. I knew that look – after all, I'd known her all her life. Kitty came to make trouble, but there is a peculiar twist to this tale: she left, having stirred us up, but resolving everything.

Kitty never comes to Old Romney unless to attend church. Like Lucy and me, she has chores which keep her at home. So, when she walked into the rectory kitchen without even having the decency to knock and with a malicious look in her eyes, it seemed as if my heart stopped beating for a moment. Then those last words spoken to Little Lucy crashed about in my head and I knew Lucy had told Kitty. *It's Reverend Edward Kenelm I'll be marrying.*

"Greetings, Goodwife Beth," Kitty said, seating herself at the kitchen table. "Hello Mary."

"Funny time to come calling, Miss Kitty." Beth also sensed disruption to our peaceful existence. "We're about to serve dinner. The men are waiting."

"Oh, I'll keep out of the way," Kitty declared. "Aren't you going to say hello, Mary?"

"I'll say hello, but aren't you needed in the kitchen at Wheelsgate?" I responded, my tone tart.

"Not today." Kitty beamed – a smile soon wiped from her face when Beth thumped a heavy pan of stew on the table.

"Then you can share Mary's dinner once the men are settled," Beth said. "You're here for a reason, no doubt, and there will be time to hear it soon enough. Now, if you don't mind, you're in my way sitting there."

I placed two plates on the table and Kitty stood, stepping back towards the doorway. "A plate of dinner would be welcome," she said. "But I thought Mary would be eating with the gents."

It had started – the trickle of gossip passing from Deanes Farm to Wheelsgate, gathering momentum and coming to flood the rectory. I felt as if all colour had drained from my face and my body stiffened. No words came.

"What nonsense you speak," Beth responded. "We all know our place here."

If I could have flashed her a look of gratitude without my sister noticing, I would have done so. Goodwife Beth was proving a staunch ally.

"Take the dinner through, Mary," Beth ordered. Somehow my arms moved forward to take the plates and my body turned to begin the short walk from kitchen to front parlour. "Then back for the bread," the cook reminded me. She knew my mind was frozen and all routines lost to me.

"Back for the bread," I repeated, setting off along the short hallway.

Nudging the parlour door, I stepped into the room. Both men turned to face me, their smiles turning to confusion. In turn, my face fell as I sensed Kitty had followed and stood framed in the doorway behind me.

"I've brought the bread," she said. "Good day, gentlemen. I'm Kitty, Mary's sister."

My rector and Mister Bridgeman murmured their greetings.

"I mustn't disturb your meal, but I had to come, Reverend Kenelm, and congratulate you on your plans to marry Mary."

Silence fell upon us – all polite murmurings cut dead. My heart slammed and my gaze fell on Edward's face to see a look of horror flash across it, followed by – could it be? – revulsion. Those first reactions passed, to be replaced with a stillness, then I saw that his mouth twitched a little, as if there were words to be uttered, but none came. Our eyes met and I saw none of the kindness – none of the affection – shown in the past. We four remained frozen: the men seated, me with a plate in each hand, and Kitty at my shoulder. My gaze remained fixed on my rector and his on me.

Then he began to open his mouth, and I knew he had found a way to dismiss Kitty's congratulations and to place me on a path leading to a lifetime of humiliation. Yet as the rector uttered those first words, Mister Bridgeman's voice cut through them, and we all turned to look at him.

"Kitty – a pleasure to meet you, but you are mistaken – I am the lucky man Mary has agreed to marry!" He smiled a smile which encompassed us all and his blue eyes crinkled at the edges.

Stunned, I felt relief flood through my body. The curate had spared my embarrassment, but what would the rector do? I turned, silently offering the chance for my faith in him to be restored but knowing it was not to be.

I was not surprised by his response: "My dear Kitty, how good of you to come bearing your best wishes. I was about to tell Mister Bridgeman I have found a cottage that will suit him and Mary nicely. I can only hope your sister will delay her marriage until I have found another maid. But we can discuss that later. Mary, can we have our dinner, please. Goodwife Beth will be venting her displeasure if we eat a cold meal."

I stepped forward, placing the plates on the table, then left the room. Kitty – hot on my heels – expressed her fury on our return to the kitchen. "Lucy got herself in a right muddle. I told her it must be wrong. Mary marrying a rector – how could that be true? But she told me... Now she's made me look stupid."

"If you look stupid, then you've only got yourself to blame," Beth pointed out. "If Mary had news to share, then she'd tell you herself. What must the men think of you barging in here?"

I hadn't uttered a word. How could I be anything but struck dumb by the compassion shown by Mister Bridgeman? He had spared my embarrassment in front of Kitty but placed himself in an impossible situation by claiming we were to marry. How would we undo his kind words? Somehow, I found myself sitting at the kitchen table, with my sister believing I was to marry the curate, and Beth ignorant of the scene in the parlour.

"So now you know your sister is to marry our Mister Bridgeman," Beth stated. *Of course, she must have followed and heard what was said.* "Perhaps you should have waited until Mary saw fit to tell you the news. But now you've heard it, then I'd like to think you've come to offer your good wishes."

"Well done, Mary," Kitty reacted in her off-hand manner.

I moved my mouth and somehow responded with murmured thanks.

"I've got to get home, so you can serve your own dinner." Beth bustled towards the door. "Still staying, are you, Kitty?"

"I've got to get back," my sister replied. "I've lost my appetite."

They left together and I sat with a bowl of stew before me. The rich aroma filled my nostrils, streaming into my throat until, gagging on it, I raced to the back door and outside to vomit. Afterwards, I stood for a moment, bent low, my hands on my knees, trying to breathe slowly. Then I straightened and headed back to the well, where I scooped handfuls of fresh water from a bucket and cleansed my mouth.

On my return to the kitchen, I tipped my uneaten meal back into the pot. Once cold it would go on the stone shelf in the larder and make the filling for the next day's pie. My slice of bread I kept to nibble on. After that, I had no choice but to return to the men and collect their plates. It was only as I walked from the kitchen to the parlour that I began to wonder how they had filled that awkward time – forced to be in each other's company after the dreadful scene.

"Mary, we were just speaking about the new baby born at Agney Court and the baptism," Mister Bridgeman said as I entered the room. How kind of him to attempt to put me at ease.

I smiled the best I could, but kept my eyes lowered. "A girl, I think?"

"A bonny girl," he confirmed.

I took their plates, while avoiding looking directly at either of them, and backed away. "Can I get you anything else?"

They declined, thankfully. I retreated to the back of the house, glad to be spared any further embarrassment. Once the kitchen had been tidied and the laundry turned to catch the warm rays of late September sunshine, I took a light shawl and walked past the vegetable garden to the churchyard, hoping to spend time on my own and to find some peace within my troubled mind.

I meandered past the grave of the rector's wife and child – *how foolish of me to think that I could ever replace her.* Then I paused at my parents' grave – *how thankful I am that you have been spared seeing your daughter act so foolishly.* Finally, I settled on the grass in the southeastern corner, not far from the dyke and the willows, and gazed across the pasture towards Hope.

Of course, sitting there alone with no one to guide me, I could not hope to resolve any of my troubles. I could not begin to picture a time when I might live alongside the rector as his maid but with all affection cast aside. And what about the marriage to Mister Bridgeman – Avery – which seemed to be settled? How would he undo his generous words when he could have no intention of marrying me?

I sat, mulling over this and that, until I realised that Davey had unwittingly come up with my answer when he said I could always have a home with them. "It is the only way," I muttered to myself. "Both the men will be relieved to see the back of me, and Lucy will be delighted. I will be nothing more than her maid, but it will be no less than my place at the rectory."

"I had no idea where to find you, but something led me here."

I hadn't heard anyone approach and turned to see Avery smiling down at me. He sat on the grass beside me, and said, "Oh Mary, if I could have saved you that scene."

"But you did. At least you saved me from Kitty's scorn." I paused and gazed into the distance, allowing my eyes to glaze over. Then I continued, keeping my face turned away from him, "It is best that I go to my sister, Lucy. I cannot think of any other way to spare you."

"You can go to Lucy, or I have another idea," Avery replied. "Shall we sit here and talk for a while?"

Avery

Just three weeks ago, Mary answered the door of the rectory and welcomed me in. From my first hours there, I wondered who she was, sensing her position was not as lowly as maid, or as elevated as family member. Then it dawned on me that she had fallen in love with Edward Kenelm, but I could not fathom if the feelings were returned.

Living under the same roof, I pondered on their relationship. I soon realised that whenever work took me away for any length of time, Mary would be flustered on my return, blushing prettily as she fell over her words. At the same time, the rector seemed brusque and defensive. Whether he was in love with her or not, I felt certain that he was taking advantage of her affection. As house guest and curate, I found Mary to be good-natured and hard-working. As a man, I noticed her clear skin, soft, blonde hair and bright eyes. She had supported the rector during his time of grieving, but now her passion for him left her vulnerable.

In those three weeks, I learnt that Mary had some education, she was reliable and sensible, polite and considerate. I admired her more every day. Edward Kenelm, however, I liked less and less every day. His dedication to his flock appeared unpredictable – one moment his attention faultless, the next sloppy. More and more he began to strut about the place, and any woman younger than thirty was an object for him to appraise. Twice he rode to New Romney, and I believed that a woman he met there had taken his fancy.

When Mary's sister stood at the parlour door and announced Mary and Edward were to marry, I knew there had been some terrible mistake, and my first reaction was to spare her humiliation.

Neither Edward nor I mentioned the scene when Mary and Kitty left. Instead, we studiously ignored it and spoke of mundane matters. He knew there was no romance between Mary and me, and he knew I was aware of his own mistreatment of her.

Afterwards, when I had given myself time to consider it, I realised that to marry her would be no hardship. She was in love with another man but had already seen his cruel side, and we had developed an easy friendship since my arrival at Old Romney. A mutual affection, even love, could follow.

When I found Mary in the churchyard, my arms ached to be wrapped around her, to offer some comfort. Instead, I sat beside her, and began carefully, "I do not pretend that we are in love with each other, but we *can* marry..."

"Marry? But why would you want to?"

"Because you are good and kind, and I know you would support me in my work." I turned and looked at her, although she still gazed ahead. "Because I think you are lovely," I added.

"You are kind. Too kind." She began to pluck at long strands of grass, gathering them together. "What will he say?"

"He will say nothing because he knows he has treated you badly and will be grateful if no one knows about it."

"Beth knows."

"Beth will not want to make trouble."

Things were going well, so I decided to be honest with Mary. "I realised very soon after taking this role that the rector and I will not work well together." She turned to look at me then and I saw her blue eyes were filled with unshed tears. "I am grateful for his offer of a home and work, and thought I would stay for a year or two – this much I owed him. However, I do not *have* to stay here. This visitation from Canterbury has highlighted the need for members of the clergy in so many local parishes, and I could ask to be moved to where I could do better good. Although I was ordained for such a short time before leaving Newchurch, I am determined to prove myself worthy of the role again. In time I can find a position as curate elsewhere."

I paused, allowing her a moment to reflect on my words. Mary was a young woman on the verge of fleeing her home and work, and I knew she deserved better than being a housemaid for her younger sister.

"You would leave Old Romney for me? To spare me the shame?"

"I would." Once more I waited before continuing. "I have nothing to offer but my willingness to treat you kindly, and I cannot take you away from here today or tomorrow, but I can promise to do my best over the coming months."

"Away from Romney Marsh?" Her voice rose, as she explained, "I can't leave my sisters."

"Nay, away from Old Romney. Away from him."

"I see. You're so kind and I don't deserve it."

We sat in companionable silence for a little longer. Only this morning, neither of us had considered marriage – at least not with each other. The warmth of summer days had passed, and as we watched water moving sluggishly in the nearby ditch and slender leaves falling from the willows, I saw that Mary was beginning to grow chilly. She rubbed her arms, then stood.

"I have work to do, but thank you. Thank you for everything." She looked directly at me and gave a weak smile. "You should not commit yourself to marriage just to save me. Let's think about this and speak again later. I know there is so little time now the words have been said."

"Shall we speak again today? After Evensong?"

"After Evensong," she confirmed before turning away.

I believe Mary returned to the house, and how difficult that must have been for her, not knowing where he was, or what might pass between them if the rector knew them to be alone. From the churchyard I went into St Clement's and sat quietly, trying to empty my mind of the thoughts which tumbled about. While I breathed in the scent of ancient stone and wood, a sense of calm settled on me, and my next steps became clear. Whether Mary decided to marry me or not, I knew I should go to Newchurch to seek the advice of my old friend the rector. After that, I would write to Archbishop Parker and ask to be considered for a position in another parish.

As I had said to Mary, it would take time for me first to prove my worth here in Old Romney and then be approved to move to another parish. I wondered if she could bear to wait all those months, perhaps a year. For now, I could only wait for Mary's decision.

I spent a couple of hours visiting families living on outlying farms, but afterwards I could not have recalled what we spoke about or even the purpose of my visit. Then, back at the rectory, I fetched the axe and put all my efforts into chopping wood for the fire – a satisfying task.

The rector and I ate supper together in the parlour and studiously avoided any talk of my impending marriage before preparing for Evensong.

Later, I found Mary in the garden, swathed in a thick shawl and watching the sun set.

"Are you still offering to marry me?" she asked as I approached, without even turning to look at me.

"I am."

"Then I accept and with gratitude." Mary turned now and our eyes met. She attempted a smile, but I knew it was too early to be feeling celebratory.

"I've been thinking about writing to Archbishop Parker to ask for another position when he is satisfied that I have spent enough time here under our rector's supervision," I told her. "I can only hope the archbishop will show some compassion for my unusual choices over the past year. But if I am to follow my chosen path in the Church, then it will take time before we can leave Old Romney."

"I understand."

"Could you bear it? To remain here?"

"I could bear it for a while," she said. "If there is a cottage as he said. If we didn't have to live at the rectory."

"We must not live at the rectory, not for a moment longer than we have to," I answered, my voice becoming more forceful than intended.

"And once we are married, then you must not continue as his maid. We will be poor, I cannot deny it, but perhaps you could take in sewing or work elsewhere?"

"I would gladly do that." I noticed a sparkle in her eyes as Mary began to picture a life away from the rectory. Then she smiled, a smile with real warmth to it. "Thank you, Mister Bridgeman. Avery. Thank you."

"I'll tell the rector it is all settled between us," I told her. Then I reached forward to take her hand. "This may not be the usual way to become betrothed, but I have a feeling that neither of us will regret it."

Mary

Today is my wedding day. Avery and I will be married in Newchurch by the rector of that parish. I could not bear Reverend Kenelm to take the ceremony, and he has not been invited. Soon, Avery will call for me and we will walk there together, taking no heed of the traditions which say we should arrive separately at the church. We will tread our own path, Avery says, and he is right. As long as we are honest and caring towards each other, then our marriage will be strong.

When I think back to that scene in the parlour, when Kitty announced I was to marry the rector, my thoughts drift to Little Lucy and a feeling of unease settles in my stomach. She only repeated what I had told her. When Kitty was put in her place, she blamed Lucy for getting it wrong and one day soon, she will vent her fury at Lucy. When I am married, I am determined to go to Deanes Farm and share my news with Lucy, but also to tell her the truth of what happened that day when Avery and I agreed to marry. My youngest sister is a married woman now and she does not deserve to be made to feel foolish.

She never did deserve it, but Kitty was always harsh with her.

There was no cottage for Avery and I – the rector's words were nothing but waffle, as they so often are. Instead, Margery, a great friend of my mother, and her husband, Jed, have offered us the room their son and his wife used for some years after they married. As Margery brushes my hair, and I smooth the woollen skirt of my best dress, my gaze roams to the newly-completed patchwork bedcover. Rays of weak November sun shine through leaded windowpanes, and a shaft of light falls across the scraps of material, each one holding a memory.

"Your mother would be proud," Margery says.

"I hope so."

"I know so. He's a good man."

"Thank you. Thank you for all of this," I gesture to the room. "And for coming to see us married."

"I'm glad to be a part of it. You'll be off soon, to some other parish. Brenzett, or St Marys, it seems. Until then, Jed and I are pleased to have you here."

"The archbishop seems eager for Avery to be placed somewhere else."

Voices outside alert us to its being time to leave. We'll make a small wedding party. Like Lucy, I'll share the news afterwards.

"Time to go," Margery leads the way back into the kitchen as the men enter the cottage.

Avery carries a small bunch of winter roses which he presents to me. I lift them to my face and inhale the rich scent, then smile.

"Ready to be married?" he asks, offering his hand.

"I'm ready," I say.

The roads to Newchurch will be rutted, and the wind will play havoc with my hair, but the sky is a glorious, clear blue and the hedgerows are rich with berries. As we set off, an odd rhythmic hum fills the air, and we all pause to watch a flight of swans beating a path through the sky. These loyal birds mate for life, and their appearance fills my heart with joy. Together, Avery and I gaze upwards, in awe of the magnificent swans, and I know their appearance is a good omen for our life together.

The end

Thanks

Special thanks to Jackie Halls who inspired Mary's patchwork.

With thanks to Chris Finn-Kelcey and Jonathan Finn-Kelcey for sharing their knowledge of Old Romney and Midley with me.

Thank you to everyone who supports my writing through buying my novels and attending workshops, and to the local stockists.

I am so grateful to those who spend hours helping me with the editing and proof reading. Every error you spot helps me to improve the final draft.

Many thanks to my family and friends who are so understanding about the huge amount of time I need to spend creating novels, workshops and talks.

Midley

Midley – The Settlers
Lydd & Midley 11th century
(2024)

Midley – Five Gold Coins
Canterbury & Midley 14th century
(2024)

Midley - Abandoned
Brookland, Midley, Old Romney 16th century
(2025)

Coming up…

Midley – At War (working title)
Lydd & Midley 1940s
(estimated publication autumn 2025)

www.emmabattenauthor.com
email:batten.em@outlook.com
Facebook: Emma Batten Author
Instagram: emma.batten.author

Printed in Dunstable, United Kingdom